Darker

Demons

By

Beth McCue

Oceans Ending Publishing

Published by Oceans Ending Publishing
North Charleston, South Carolina

This is a work of fiction. Names, characters, businesses,
places, events and incidents are either the products of the
author's imagination or used in a fictitious manner. Any
resemblance to actual persons, living or dead, or actual
events is purely coincidental.

CHAPTER 1

Awakening, Alexandra is engulfed in darkness so dense she can't tell if her eyes are open or shut. Head and heart pounding, she reaches up, probing. Her hand brushes against something; something soft and wet.

Stifling the scream threatening to escape from her throat, she tries to move her legs. There is plenty of space to move them from side to side but when she tries to lift them, they hit an obstacle.

The world is black but slowly lightening.

"Think Alex, what's the last thing you remember?" she asks herself in a hollow-sounding voice.

She remembers a dark street; walking with Jake. They had left the movie before it was over and headed downtown for a late dinner. They agreed the storyline of the so-called "based on real events" film was implausible; some nonsense about ghosts and demons roaming the streets of New Orleans.

She could picture Jake's face as they passed under the gas lamp in front of their favorite restaurant. His dark brown eyes were crinkling at the corners as they recalled one of the more absurd scenes from the film.

And then...nothing. The pounding in her head is easing up a little. She tries to sit up but discovers something holding her back. Turning her head she finds she can only move it an inch or two in either direction.

Blinding light is coming from above her. Unable to shield her eyes, she squeezes them shut, but the light penetrates her eyelids. She has the sensation of being touched but can't feel anything solid. It is more an idea of touching, being caressed by a breath.

Her body begins to respond to the touch. Trying to fight it off in her confused and weakened state is impossible.

Strange scenes play out behind her eyelids. She sees Jake but not Jake. His eyes are an odd shape and bulge out of his head. He is laughing.

She sees herself spread-eagled on a metallic platform; something holding her down. Around her neck is a metal choker fastened to the platform with a heavy chain.

Then Jake is on top of her…and she is screaming, and screaming.

Reawakening, she hears the birds outside her window. Her neck feels raw. The dream has left her badly shaken. Realizing she has no memory of the previous night, she feels the beginnings of a panic attack.

Throwing back the covers she gasps as her feet hit the floor. Terrible cramps grip her insides and she doubles over in pain. Collapsing back on the bed she tries to catch her breath.

After a few moments, the pain subsides and she is able to stand then walk to the bathroom. Gazing at her reflection she feels bewildered as if the woman staring back is a stranger.

"Where were we last night?" she asks the woman; no reply.

Showering in the soothing, warm water helps bring her back to reality but doesn't trigger any recollections of the previous night. Her phone begins ringing as she is toweling off. It is her boss wanting to know where the hell she is.

"But it's Sunday. Why would I come to work on a Sunday?"

"Well, you must have had one crazy weekend. It's Monday morning and you are supposed to be here helping me prepare for our presentation tomorrow," her boss Caitlin scolds.

"Oh geez, I'm so sorry. I don't know what happened. I will be there as soon as I can."

"Are you sure you are all right? Your voice sounds kind of hoarse."

"Yes, yes. I'm fine. I'll see you in a bit." Throwing open her closet door she is dismayed to see nothing but tailored clothes in neutral shades.

"Why do I have all these boring outfits? These are not my taste at all." Or are they?

Once again she has the overwhelming feeling of inhabiting a stranger's body.

Pushing hanger after hanger aside she finally comes across a peacock blue, silk dress.

"This is more like it," she says, the soft fabric sliding between her fingers, giving her chills.

Slipping the dress over her head she turns to admire her image. The woman in the mirror is smiling her approval.

Returning to the bathroom she pulls out her makeup drawer and begins applying lines and color to her eyelids. Puckering her lips she adds deep red lipstick.

"I didn't even know I had this color, pretty hot," she tells her reflection.

On any other day, she would put on sneakers and walk the five blocks to her office. Today, she slips on heels and pulls out her phone to arrange for an Uber pickup. By the time she locates her purse and walks downstairs her ride is waiting at the curb.

The young, male driver casts an admiring look in the rearview mirror.

"Headed to the office? It must be rough."

"How did you know I was going to the office?" Alexandra asks.

"The address you gave. It's an office building."

"Right, sorry. I had a strange weekend," Alexandra replies.

The young man grins. "I hear ya'."

The car pulls up in front of Alexandra's office and the young driver jumps out, almost before the car has stopped, to rush around and open the door for her. He reaches out. She takes his hand. Startled by the sudden feeling of heat, she jerks her hand back.

The driver only smiles and bows his head. "Enjoy your day Alex," he says, winking as he walks away.

Hurrying up the steps to the front door of her office building, she is aware of the hollow sound her heels are making as they hit the bricks.

Throwing open the door, she is struck by the absence of motion. People at their desks pose like mannequins. All eyes are on her as she walks across the room to her desk.

"What is it, people? Haven't you ever seen anyone get to work a little late? Geez."

Caitlin's office door is opening, slowly. Her boss is looking at her so strangely, shaking her head.

Standing, she shouts a question at Caitlin, "What's wrong with everyone? Why are you all behaving like this?"

Caitlin has reached Alexandra's desk. She drops something-- a newspaper-- on the desk and points.

Picking it up, Alexandra sees the headline. It's about Jake. The story says his body was found late Sunday night in Woldenberg Park. The horrifying details regarding the condition of the body are too much for her. She collapses in a dead faint.

Struggling to regain consciousness is like trying to escape heaven to enter hell. As she opens her eyes the pain claws away at her brain leaving it shredded and raw.

Caitlin is leaning over her with a damp cloth, patting her forehead. There are two policemen now, one on each side of her boss.

"Alexandra, can you hear me? These men want to ask you some questions hon. Are you up to it?"

"Excuse me ma'am but, she has to answer our questions, whether she feels up to it or not."

Alexandra brushes Caitlin's hand away. "What is it you need to ask me, officer…?"

"Aaron. Officer Aaron. I'd like to know where you were last evening."

Beginning calmly, she says, "I wish I could tell you but, I can't seem to remember anything about last night. In fact, I don't remember anything after Saturday night when Jake…oh God, Jake…Jake!"

The moans coming out of her now are barely human. Unable to utter even the briefest answers to the questions being thrown at her, she just covers her face and screams, "Just leave me alone!"

Caitlin turns on the officers, shouting at them to call an ambulance. "She's hysterical. She needs medical attention now!"

That's the last thing she hears before passing out again.

Her eyes open. She sees a man in a white coat leaning over her. Behind him is Caitlin, teary-eyed, wringing her hands. There doesn't appear to be anyone else in the small room.

"Oh thank God you're awake! I was getting so worried!"

Trying to answer, her raw throat makes it impossible to do more than groan.

The doctor pats her hand and turns to Caitlin.

Taking her arm, they walk out of the room and he returns alone.

"Don't worry. It's normal for you to have difficulty talking after so much time."

She manages to get out two words, "How long?"

"You've been with us for two weeks."

Seeing the panicked expression on her face the doctor tries to reassure her. "Don't worry Alexandra. You're fine. You're going to be all right now. Try to get some rest," he says as he leaves the room.

"Rest," she thinks. "Isn't that all I have been doing for two weeks? How can I rest when I have no idea what's happening to me?"

Abruptly recalling the events leading up to her collapse, she feels her head explode with pain.

"Jake! Oh God. He's dead. He's dead and I have no clue where I was when it happened."

She sits up, frantically searching for a wastebasket or bedpan, anything able to catch the bile rising in her throat. She grabs the water pitcher too late. She buzzes for the nurse then puts her head back on the pillow, sobs shaking her body.

The nurse bustles in and cleans up the mess, replacing the soiled blanket with a fresh one. She fetches a bright blue bag and places it on Alexandra's nightstand.

"Here you go, babe. If you feel sick again, just use this here bag."

Alexandra nods her head and smiles, pointing to her throat. She hopes the nurse understands it is still difficult to speak. After patting her hand and smiling, the nurse leaves.

"Odd language for a nurse," Alexandra thinks.

Alone again, Alexandra tries to reconstruct the events which ended with her in the hospital in a coma. There is a faint memory, a whisper in her consciousness. She recalls waking up in darkness almost unable to move; then a bright, piercing light...then nothing.

The doctor and Caitlin return. He says, "I'm sending your boss home. She has been here almost constantly since we admitted you. She needs some rest before she collapses too. I'll give you two a minute alone."

Suddenly, Alexandra feels herself slipping back again, away from the present. It's like being sucked into a deep hole. Caitlin is receding until she is no more than a tiny dot in Alexandra's vision.

She is in her apartment. The hospital gown is gone.

She is dressed in jeans and a low cut silk blouse, holding two glasses of wine. She looks up and sees a man on the couch. He is smiling at her, holding out his hand to accept the glass she is offering.

She passes the wine and sits down next to him. "Are you all right babe? You're looking at me a little oddly," Jake says.

"Yes, I'm okay. I just had the weirdest feeling, though. I can't put my finger on it but…I feel like we have done this exact same thing, had this same conversation before."

"That's not really so peculiar, is it? I'm sure we have had very similar conversations in the past."

"I guess but this was different somehow. I got a really strong feeling of déjà vu."

"So, what would you like to do tonight? Do you want to see the new movie everyone is talking about, *Darker Demons*?"

"NO! Sorry, no, I heard it was terrible. Why don't we just stay home?"

"Mmm. I like the sound of that," Jake says. He puts down his wine and reaches over, grabbing Alexandra's hair, pulling her towards him. Roughly yanking her blouse over her head, he is kissing her so hard her mouth feels bruised and hot.

"What are you doing? Take it easy! You're hurting me!"

"You seemed to like it the other night with all those people watching. You kept begging me for more. Don't you remember babe?"

As Alexandra looks into his bulging eyes, she sees her own reflection surrounded by flames.

CHAPTER 2

Struggling to open her eyes, Alexandra glances around and recognizes she is back in the hospital.

"What is happening to me? Am I really awake and at the hospital or is this part of a dream?"

She wonders if she is insane, or maybe even…dead. There is nothing concrete for her to hold on to. Each time she believes she is in the "real world" she is pulled away.

"Am I even who I think I am? Does Jake exist or did I make him up?"

She is sitting up in bed, tears streaming down her face, when the nurse enters her room for the usual morning poking, prodding and temperature taking.

"How are we doing this morning? The doctor says you may be able to go home in a couple of days."

"I'm exhausted and confused and sore and grumpy."

"At least your throat is healing. The hoarseness is almost gone." Under her breath she mumbles, "Now we can hear all of your bitching."

The nurse completes her tasks, telling Alexandra the doctor would be in to visit her later in the morning. She hands Alexandra two pills. Swallowing them she is soon deeply asleep again.

When Alexandra next awakens, it is evening. A faint light is peeking through the window blinds. She reaches up to rub her eyes and realizes the IV needle is no longer in her arm.

Tossing the covers off, she heads for the closet, expecting to find the blue dress she had worn to the office; the event she believes preceded her trip to the hospital. Instead, she finds the pair of black leggings, tunic and knee-high boots she had worn on her date with Jake.

Feeling pressed for time; afraid she will pass out again, she grabs the clothes and heads for the bathroom. She turns on the light. The face in the mirror is shockingly gaunt and pale, but at least it feels like her face. She pulls her thick dark hair up into a ponytail, washes up and gets dressed.

Back in the room, she sees her purse on the bedside table. Rummaging through it, she finds her wallet. The face on the driver's license is hers, but the name, Alexandra Laveau, is not.

She feels faint, fights it off. Opening the door a crack, she peeks outside. There is no one around. She can hear noise coming from what she believes is the nurse's station located out of sight, around the corner.

Pushing harder, she looks down the hall and sees a red exit sign. She heads towards it. She reaches the door and opens it without incident. No alarms go off; she doesn't think anyone sees her leave.

The exit has led her to a set of steps attached to the outside of the building. The cool air is shocking. She races down as quickly as she can in the uncomfortable boots.

Scanning the street she is struck by the realization she has no clue where she is. Pulling out the wallet again, she finds several $20 bills. Locating her license, she checks out the address. It is the same one she remembers.

Hailing a cab, she gives the driver the address. Her building looks the same; loaded with what they call New Orleans charm. What they really mean is old and prone to flooding.

Climbing the one flight of stairs to her place, exhaustion is creeping in. "I can't wait to climb into my own bed again," she thinks, but when she reaches her apartment and attempts to put the key in the lock, it doesn't fit.

CHAPTER 3

Caitlin throws her cell phone across the room, wishing for a moment she had a heavy, old-fashioned receiver to slam down.

Infuriated by the discovery she has just made, she screams to the empty room, "Those incompetent idiots! How could they let that little bitch escape?"

She storms down the hallway to the "nurse's station." In actuality, just a desk where two young women sit with bowed heads, awaiting the wrath of Caitlin.

"What is wrong with you two? How hard was it to keep her drugged up and in her room? How could you let this happen?"

"We're sorry Miss Caitlin," the one named Joanne says meekly.

"We don't know how she could have escaped. She was completely out of it. Between the IV drugs and the pills, it was…well it was damned near impossible for her to have left on her own."

"Damned near or not, she's gone and we have no way of knowing how long ago she escaped. Did you hear anything strange? Could someone have gotten into the building and helped her?"

"No ma'am," Joanne answers. "We didn't hear a thing."

"Are you sure you two weren't having a little party here; maybe breaking into the pill supply?"

"Absolutely not! I swear we've been clean this entire time."

"I guess this is what I get for hiring a couple of prostitutes. Get your stuff and get out of my sight. And remember, if I find out you have told anyone about what went on here, I won't hesitate to blow your pretty little brains out."

The two girls grab their belongings and scurry out. Caitlin paces the hallway while waiting for Jake to arrive. She is still fuming when he finally shows up.

"All right. I'm here. Tell me what happened," Jake demands.

"Those two bimbos blew one of the easiest jobs on the planet. Alexandra is gone. She escaped."

"How can that be? She was pumped so full of drugs she could barely open her eyes. She must have had help," Jake says.

"Don't you think I asked them if they heard anything unusual? And besides, who would have helped her? No one knew she was here except the two of us and those two…those two," she says, pointing down the hallway in the direction of their exit.

"I don't know babe, but, we better figure it out in a hurry."

"Can't you do something?" Caitlin asks. "Give her another hallucination with your device?"

"No. It won't work if she's not on the IV. The drugs are what enable the brain wave altering chip to work," Jake lies. He has never told Caitlin the truth; there is no brain wave altering chip. His business is just a front.

"Great. So what do we do?"

"I don't know. Give me a minute. She won't go to the police, so we don't need to worry about that. I don't think she was really close to anyone except the two of us…and the Judge. We just need to figure out where she'll go…and get there first."

"Brilliant. How the fuck do we do that?"

"Go to her apartment. See if you can get Tom, that imbecile of a superintendent to let you in. Maybe you can find papers; a diary; a list of phone numbers, anything we can use to help us pin her down. I'll clean up here and meet you at our place later."

CHAPTER 4

Staring at the useless key in her hand, Alexandra is befuddled. Startled by the sound of someone approaching from behind, she spins around. She recognizes her friend Tom, the building superintendent. "Oh, thank goodness it's you. You scared me. What's going on here? Why doesn't my key open the door?"

"Alexandra? I thought you were…I mean you're supposed to be…not supposed to be but…"

"What? What are you trying to say?"

"I think you better come downstairs with me and I'll explain."

Reaching out for something to hold on to as her knees buckle, she feels Tom grab her before she hits the floor.

"When was the last time you had a meal? No offense but, you look awful."

"Thanks. I can't even tell you when I last ate. I vaguely remember throwing up in the hospital, but, I can't seem to remember eating."

She follows Tom down the stairs to his apartment. Sighing as she sinks down into the comfortable couch, she explains, "I'm so exhausted."

"What hospital were you in?" Tom asks. "And why were you there?"

"I'm not sure. I didn't recognize the neighborhood…but it was fairly close, only eight or nine blocks away. I don't know why I was there…it's all so muddled," her voice trails off as she looks to Tom to fill in the blank.

"I can't help you out. There are no hospitals I know of within a few blocks of here. Besides, if you were in the hospital, wouldn't the police have known about it?"

Alexandra's confusion is obvious when she asks, "Police? Are the police looking for me? Do they think I am the one who killed Jake?"

Tom holds a hand up. "Whoa! Jake isn't dead, not the Jake you were dating anyway."

"How do you know that?" Alexandra asks in an accusatory tone.

They are interrupted by someone pounding on the door. Leading Alexandra into the bedroom, Tom motions for her to be silent.

Caitlin is about to knock again when Tom flings open the door, almost toppling her over.

"May I help you?" Tom asks.

"Yes, I'm Caitlin Jensen. I was Alexandra's employer. You remember; we met one time when I was picking her up for a girl's night out."

"Yes," Tom replies, "I remember. What do you want?"

Caitlin appears taken aback by his gruff reply. "I need to get inside Alexandra's apartment and look for some papers I gave her regarding one of our clients."

"I'm sorry but I can't allow that. The police have told me no one is allowed inside until they close their investigation."

"Shit! What difference does it make if I go into her apartment? I'm not going to remove any evidence or anything."

Surprised at her bluntness, Tom answers, "She is…was a suspect in a murder investigation, in case you have forgotten. And according to you, she committed suicide. Even if the police didn't tell me not to let anyone in, I wouldn't let you in!"

Trying a different approach, Caitlin tilts her head to the side and smiles up at Tom, saying, "I won't tell anyone you broke the rules if you don't. Just let me search for my papers. I'll be out in one tiny second."

"I'm sorry, but no."

"You will regret this," Caitlin threatens as she spins on her heel and stomps off.

Slamming the door, Tom turns to find Alexandra standing in the bedroom doorway.

"Murder investigation? But you said Jake isn't dead!" Alexandra grabs the door as the room begins to tilt again, a sensation becoming all too familiar.

Tom replies, "Jake wasn't the victim. Listen, why don't I fix you something to eat and then I will tell you everything I can about what has been happening?"

"All right, but I'm craving some pizza. Do you mind?"

Tom smiles, "Mind? I guess you've forgotten our weekly pizza and cheesy movie parties."

For what feels like the first time in forever, Alexandra smiles. "Now you mention it, I think I do recall watching some really bad movies together while eating some really good pizza!"

Seated across the table from Tom enjoying the pizza and some Chianti, recent events begin to seem like a dream to Alexandra.

"I wish I could just stay here in this moment forever," she says.

"I wish you could too," Tom says, the words catching in his throat.

"So please, now will you tell me what's going on?"

"What is the last thing you remember?" Tom asks.

Alexandra shakes her head trying to clear the cobwebs.

"I can't really be sure which memories are true. The last thing I am certain of is, I saw you Saturday when I was on my way out for a jog. After that…I recall walking down Canal Street with Jake. We had gone to see that new movie, *Darker Demons*, and left before it was over. We headed to the Quarter for dinner. It was Saturday night.

"Then I woke up Monday morning feeling like someone had beaten me with a baseball bat. Caitlin called wanting to know why I was late for work. I thought she was crazy, 'It's Sunday', I said.

"She said, 'It's Monday!' and made some comment about a rough weekend and told me to hurry up and get to work."

"All right," Tom says. "So far nothing really out of the ordinary except maybe the lost day. Are you sure it actually was Monday?"

"What do you mean? Of course it was. Why would she make that up? Besides, when I got to the office, everyone was there. And the Uber driver, he said…"

"Yes? What did he say?" Tom asks.

"Come to think of it, he made a comment like, 'It must be rough,' when I said I was going to the office. It seemed a little strange but not strange enough to cause any concern. Maybe he meant it was rough because it was Sunday!"

"Okay, so tell me what happened when you arrived at the office?"

Continuing her story, Alexandra says, "It was eerily quiet. People were at their desks, but no one was saying a word. Then Caitlin came out of her office and walked over to me. She dropped a newspaper on my desk and pointed, like the ghost of Jacob Marley in *A Christmas Carol*, with that long bony finger.

"The story was about Jake's death and how…oh no, it was awful!"

"I understand, but, try to tell me what happened next."

"Okay. She showed me the newspaper story and I fainted. When I woke up there were two policemen there. They said they wanted to ask me some questions about my whereabouts Saturday night. I started telling them but when I got to the Jake part, I just lost it.

"When I woke up again, I was in the hospital…or whatever. Caitlin was there. The doctor said I had been in the hospital, in a coma, for two weeks," Alexandra says.

Tom tells her, "That's impossible. Today is Tuesday. The murder just happened on Saturday night, according to the news."

Alexandra expresses her shock at this revelation.

"You okay?" Tom asks. She nods. He continues, "Do you remember the doctor's name?"

"No. I don't feel like he ever told me his name. He never examined me or anything; just talked to me."

"I wonder if he really was a doctor," Tom says.

Alexandra looks queasy as she answers, "I don't know how much of what I recollect actually happened. Maybe he didn't even exist anywhere but in my imagination.

"Anyway, the doctor left and Caitlin came back in, started talking to me, and I must have blacked out again. The next thing I knew I was in my apartment with Jake.

We were having some wine and talking about what we were going to do. I suggested we just stay home.

"He liked the idea, but then, he grabbed me and started ripping my clothes off and..." Alexandra can see Tom's increasingly angry expression.

"It's all right. He didn't hurt me," she lies. "Then I woke up again back in the hospital."

"Is that when you finally managed to escape?"

"Escape? That's a strange way to put it but now, hearing you say it, it did feel like I was escaping. I woke up and for the first time, felt like I was truly awake. I noticed the IV needle had been pulled out; maybe I did it in my sleep. I got up. I was shaky, but, I managed to get dressed. After that, I just left. I didn't see anyone on my way to the exit."

"What did the hallway look like?" Tom asks. "Did you notice anything strange, out of the ordinary?"

"No, no I don't think so. It was just a hallway. I...wait; I remember there were no other doorways; it was like mine was the only room. I thought it was peculiar but I was so desperate to get out of there, I didn't give it much thought. Then I hailed a cab...and here I am."

"All right. Do you think you are ready to hear my story? It might be difficult for you."

"I'm ready. Nothing could be worse than the hell I have already been through."

"Last Saturday, I was sitting on my couch watching the local news at 11. I jumped when your picture appeared over the anchor's shoulder. The story was about the death of Caitlin's husband..."

Tom gives her an awkward glance and continues, "He reported they had a suspect, Alexandra Dumont. He said police believed you had been having an affair with the Judge and when he refused to leave Caitlin, you killed him. They found your car later, pulled over on the Crescent City Connection. The reporter said no body was found, but, it was still possible you had jumped off the bridge."

"Where would they get a story like that? That's nonsense! The Judge and I were friends, I would never…this is unreal."

"They got the story from Caitlin. She told the police you had called her and asked her to meet you in the office, claiming you had something urgent to talk about.

"She stated she had driven to the office but it was deserted. She then returned home and discovered her husband's body. He'd been shot. At least, that was her version of events.

"Then, she went on, her phone started ringing. Supposedly, it was you on the other end and you were hysterical. 'She seemed to have completely lost her mind' was the way Caitlin put it. She said you apologized for everything before telling her you were about to kill yourself. She called the police and told them what I just told you. At the crime scene, they found your locket."

Alexandra reaches up to touch her naked throat where the locket normally rested.

"They also found your fingerprints on a glass and other items in the house."

"What if it's true? What if I did kill the Judge? I feel as if I am losing my mind," Alexandra says.

"Why don't you try and get some sleep?" Tom says.

"You can use my bed. I'll sleep on the couch. We can talk some more in the morning; figure out our next move."

"Our next move?"

Tom nods. "You didn't think I was going to let you go through this alone, did you?"

CHAPTER 5

Reaching over Jake's sleeping body Caitlin removes a cigarette from the gold case the Judge had given her on their 10th wedding anniversary.

Pulling the covers down to expose Jake's chest, Caitlin strokes his warm flesh, remembering when they had first met.

She and the Judge were planning a party on their yacht, *The Biltmore*, named for their wedding venue. Caitlin personally issued the invitation to Alexandra and she asked if she could bring a guest; some new man she was dating.

"Sure," Caitlin said. "I didn't know you were dating anyone. Tell me about him."

"His name is Jake. He's a technology geek. He has his own company built around an invention of his; some sort of chip they implant to help people with depression. I don't really understand it when he starts explaining the technical details."

"He sounds interesting," Caitlin replied, thinking the opposite.

Arriving for the party a little late, Alexandra and Jake were jogging down the dock when Caitlin laid eyes on him for the first time. She gasped, causing the woman next to her to ask, "Are you all right, hon?"

"Yes...I just. Yes. I'm fine," she said.

She rushed to the top of the steps to greet the couple. Alexandra introduced them. Jake reached out to shake her hand and she felt her face flush. She felt naked, vulnerable, as she smiled and took his hand.

"It's very nice to meet you. Alexandra has told me many wonderful things about you," Caitlin gushed.

Jake raised her hand to his lips. "I've heard many tales about you as well," he said with a sly grin.

Later, as the Judge and Alexandra were talking, Caitlin saw her husband glance over to where she and Jake were engaged in an animated discussion. Touching her cheek, she sensed it was hot with color.

She rested her hand lightly on Jake's arm. He leaned in to hear what she was saying. She looked up and noticed Alexandra glaring in their direction.

"I think I have monopolized you long enough. Alexandra is looking lonely," Caitlin said, reluctantly.

She started to walk away and felt Jake grab her arm.

"Meet me tomorrow night at the Hilton downtown."

"I can't...I can't." She pulled her arm away and hurried over to Alexandra.

"I think it's time Jake and I headed out," Alexandra said, somewhat sharply."I know he has a busy day ahead of him tomorrow."

She waved Jake over and the two of them said their goodnights.

"Interesting young man, don't you think?" the Judge asked.

Caitlin nodded, replying, "I don't know what a man like that sees in our little Alexandra."

"Hey, babe. Why are you awake?" Jake reaches out and removes Caitlin's cigarette from between her fingers.

"I thought I asked you not to smoke in bed."

"I know. I'm just nervous knowing Alexandra is out there somewhere. We should have killed her like I said," she grumbles.

Taking her hand, he kisses each finger, telling her not to think about it.

"Stop worrying. Our plan is going to work out just fine."

"Why were you so insistent we keep her alive in the first place? Do you still have feelings for her?"

"Don't talk crazy babe. You know you're the only one I want," Jake says, hoping Caitlin won't detect the lie underneath.

"There is one thing that would help me relax and fall asleep," Caitlin says in a voice wet with desire.

CHAPTER 6

Waking in the unfamiliar surroundings of Tom's bedroom, Alexandra feels a moment of panic; terrified she is trapped in another hallucination. She hears Tom rattling around in the kitchen and feels the dead weight lift off her chest.

"Hey. Why didn't you wake me up?" she asks, still groggy.

"You needed your rest. Do you feel up for some breakfast?"

"Sure, just let me get freshened up first," she answers. "Is there any chance you could sneak into my apartment and get me some clean clothes? Those clothes I found in the hospital…the facility, whatever; I think they are a little gamey."

"Yes, of course. I managed to get in there yesterday without a problem, and…" His expression makes it obvious he has said more than he intended.

"You've been in my apartment. Why?" Alexandra asks, not unkindly.

"I don't know exactly. Something about being in the apartment made me feel closer to you, almost as if you were there with me." Tom shrugs his shoulders. "I sound like some insane stalker, huh?"

"No, you sound like a caring friend."

She stands on tiptoe to give him a kiss on the cheek. "Thank you."

Reining in the urge to gather her up in his arms, he replies, "No worries. Go on and take your shower."

While she is occupied, Tom walks up the stairs to her apartment; carefully checking to be sure he is alone. He unlocks the door and steps over the threshold.

Opening Alexandra's closet he is overwhelmed by the aroma of her jasmine perfume.

He picks out a pair of dove gray pants and a blue sweater. He approaches her dresser as if it was an altar. Opening the top drawer, he sees her silk underwear and blushes. He can't bring himself to sort through it and just grabs a handful.

He finds an overnight bag perched on a shelf in the closet and puts the clothes, underwear and a few articles he feels may be important into the bag. Slowly opening the door and checking again for any unwelcome visitors, he exits.

Returning to his apartment, he leaves the bag on the bed and goes into the kitchen to finish making breakfast.

He calls out, "Hey. Are you almost ready? Your breakfast awaits."

Alexandra enters the kitchen and laughs when she sees Tom's stunned expression.

"Your hair, all that beautiful black hair. What did you do??"

"Sorry to disappoint you but, I thought I needed some type of disguise. I'm going to bleach it too if you will go to the corner and pick up some supplies for me. It doesn't look that bad, does it?" she asks, reaching up and rubbing her now-exposed neck.

"Actually, you look beautiful. Your neck is...never mind, you look good," he says, abruptly turning back to his breakfast preparations.

"Everything smells wonderful. I'm starving. What are we having?"

"Nothing exotic; just scrambled eggs, bacon, and toast. What's your coffee choice? We have vanilla, hazelnut, cinnamon or just plain super strong."

"I think…cinnamon."

Seated at Tom's table enjoying her meal, Alexandra feels her body finally beginning to relax. The muscles in her neck that had been coiled like a snake loosen, allowing her shoulders to return to their normal position. She lifts her head and smiles warmly at Tom.

"Thank you for this; for everything. I've never thanked you properly for all the little things you have done for me over the years. I'm sorry for that."

Tom makes a sweeping gesture with his hand, attempting to brush away the moment.

"Crazy girl. You don't ever have to thank me," he says, jumping up from the table. "So, what's next?"

"I need to find a way to clear my name. I wonder why Jake and Caitlin didn't just kill me. Why keep me alive? They must have known there was a risk, a small one I know, but a risk I would wake up and escape."

"So you think it was the two of them working together?" Tom asks.

"Yes, I'm afraid I do. The last thing I remember is being with Jake. If he wasn't involved, then why wouldn't he tell the police the truth; that I was with him Saturday night?

"And, whoever was helping Caitlin must have been able to control my thoughts somehow…create those hallucinations. That's sort of what Jake's business is all about, controlling people's minds.

"Also, I haven't wanted to admit this to myself, but I'm fairly certain Jake and Caitlin are having an affair. It's the only scenario that makes sense. They must have decided things would be less complicated with the Judge and me out of the picture.

"They kill the Judge, take his money and run off to some tropical island. I guess they thought pinning his death on me was the perfect way to be rid of both of us.

"I'd love to check out the 'hospital' I was in and see if they left any evidence behind," she says

Tom offers his opinion. "I doubt they would have been careless enough to do that, and, they may be watching the place hoping you will come back."

"You're probably correct," Alexandra says.

"What did you say?" Tom asks, startled.

"I said you're probably correct. Why? Was I talking quietly?"

"No, but, I swear it sounded like you were speaking a different language...sort of like French."

"I don't speak French," Alexandra replies. "In fact, the only language I speak is English."

"I must be imagining things," Tom answers. "Why don't you make up that list of supplies for me while I clean up in here?"

"Are you sure you don't want me to help? You did all the work making breakfast."

"I'm sure," Tom insists.

CHAPTER 7

Caitlin wakes up alone. Jake is gone. She rolls over and buries her face in his pillow, greedily taking in his aroma. She lingers awhile remembering their lovemaking from the night before.

Thinking out loud, she says, "I've never felt like this before; like I would die without him. What has he done to me?"

Gazing at herself in the mirror, she has the eerie feeling she is not alone in her own body. It is not the first time she has felt it.

The ringing phone startles her. She jumps, dropping her dress to the floor of the closet. Ignoring the phone, she leans over to pick it up. Something tucked behind a pair of Jake's shoes catches her eye. She is down on all fours reaching for it when Jake suddenly reappears.

"Now that's a pretty sight!" he says. "Are you looking for something babe?"

"I...I lost an earring. I thought it might have fallen under here," she lies, reluctant to tell him the truth; what she had been reaching for was a gun.

"Did you find it?" he asks, crouching down to help in the search. He begins moving things around as if looking for the earring.

"No. Don't worry about it. They were cheap earrings anyway," she says. "So what are you doing back here? I thought you were already at work."

"I was, but I was worried about you," Jake lies.

"That's so thoughtful, so not like you," she says.

Jake's face darkens for a moment and Caitlin braces for a verbal blow.

"Now is that any way to talk to the love of your life?" he says, his face returning to its normal expression.

Caitlin goes to him and they embrace. He kisses her then pushes away saying, "I've got to get to work. Save it for later, okay?"

In truth, he suddenly feels disgusted by her touch. He turns and leaves the apartment. Caitlin is distracted and doesn't notice the gun is now gone.

"What was that about?" she wonders.

Finished dressing and primping, she leaves the apartment and walks several blocks to her car. She is careful never to park too near the building where Jake has rented their rendezvous spot.

Once home, she checks the phone for messages while she feeds the dog. There are several. One is from the funeral home asking her to stop by and finalize the arrangements for the Judge's cremation. Another is from an old college friend who has heard about the murder. "Probably wants the juicy details," she thinks scornfully.

Loud knocking on the door interrupts her thoughts. It is a detective accompanied by a uniformed officer. The detective, whose name is Thibodeaux, is the one who had questioned her the night of the murder. Caitlin is repelled by the big man who smells of late night Bourbon Street.

"Mrs. Jensen, ma'am. May we come in?" he asks.

"Yes of course," she answers. Leading them to her living room, she sits down on one of the pristine, white couches, grimacing as the detective seats himself on the other.

The detective says, "There are a few discrepancies in your story I want to clear up if you have time."

Caitlin calmly answers, "Of course. What is it you would like to know?"

"You told us Miss Dumont and your husband, Judge Jensen, had been having an affair. Do you have any idea how long it had been going on?"

"No, I have no idea. The first I heard of it was the night Alexandra murdered my husband."

"Do you know Miss Dumont's boyfriend, Jake Hollings?'

Feeling icicles forming on her spine, Caitlin answers, "Yes. Alexandra brought him to one of my parties. Why?"

"Please just answer the questions Mrs. Jensen," the detective says, now sounding harsh. "Were you and Miss Dumont having an affair?"

Caitlin's reaction is genuine. She is stunned. "What on earth are you talking about? We were friends...I thought we were friends. She worked for me; that's all. We never...who told you this?" she demands to know.

"We received an anonymous call last night from someone who claimed they had spoken to Miss Dumont. She allegedly told this person the two of you had planned the murder of your husband so you could leave the country and start a new life together, but you had a change of heart. She claimed you wanted to keep all the money for yourself, so you set her up."

"It was Jake, wasn't it? That bastard!"

"Calm down Mrs. Jensen. As I said, it was an anonymous tip. We were unable to trace the call."

"Oh please. Who else could it have been? Did he also tell you he and I were having an affair? No! I didn't think so!"

Caitlin grabs her mouth as if trying to shut herself up. "I didn't mean that. I don't know what I'm saying. I…please, may I call my lawyer?"

Detective Thibodeaux holds up his hand to silence her as he answers his ringing phone. "Yes, I understand. Thanks."

He disconnects and turns to Caitlin. "Ma'am, you will have to come with us. We are going to book you for the murder of your husband. You'll be permitted to call your lawyer after we get to the station."

Breaking down, Caitlin asks, "But it's just his word. How can you believe him?"

"I'm afraid it's not just anyone's word. We obtained a search warrant based on the tip and other evidence. We visited your office this morning. We found the murder weapon in your desk drawer. We spoke to some of your staff and they confirmed your marital relationship had become very rocky. One woman claimed to have heard you threatening your husband recently," he concludes.

Caitlin holds her throbbing head in her hands. "This can't be happening," she says.

CHAPTER 8

Impatiently glancing at the clock on the kitchen wall, Alexandra wonders what is keeping Tom. The drugstore is only around the corner. Paranoia is starting to creep in when she finally hears his key in the lock.

He has his arms full of bags as he enters and kicks the door closed with his foot.

"Sorry it took so long but, I wanted to go to a store away from the neighborhood; somewhere they don't know me. Can't be too careful," he explains.

Alexandra agrees and asks what all of the additional bags are.

"Food! I wasn't really prepared for company and there isn't much here to eat…or drink."

"That was sweet of you," Alexandra says, "but I don't know how long I'm going to be here. The police will eventually discover I didn't commit suicide and come looking for me."

"No matter how long it is, we have to eat," he says.

Throwing her arms around his waist and burying her head in his chest, she sighs heavily.

"Thank you for everything you have done. I'm so sorry I'm disrupting your life this way."

Tom swallows the lump in his throat and tells her, "No need to be sorry. No need at all."

"All right," Alexandra says as she wipes the tears from her eyes. "I better get moving if I want to be a blond anytime soon."

Occupying himself putting away the groceries and cleaning up the apartment, he's unaware how much time has passed. He turns around when he hears Alexandra behind him.

"Wow!" he says.

Blushing, she reaches up and runs her fingers through her newly-blond, short hair.

"Really? It looks okay?" she asks.

"If by okay, you mean drop-dead gorgeous, then yes, it looks okay."

"Thanks," she replies. "How about we have some lunch then figure out some kind of plan?"

"Sounds good to me," Tom says.

During lunch, Alexandra questions Tom about the police investigation.

"Did they ask you any questions about me, about us?" she wants to know.

"Yes. They came here on Sunday demanding to be let into your apartment. They asked me a few things; wanted to know how well we knew each other. I told them we were friends, but, I didn't really know much about you. I told them you grew up in the convent on Dauphine Street and you went to college in New York."

"That's it?" Alexandra asks.

"Honestly," Tom says, "I don't know much more than that. I did tell them we had pizza together once a week."

"Didn't they want to know about my personality or anything?" she asks.

"They did ask me if I believed you were having an affair with Judge Jensen. I told them absolutely not."

"Is that the truth?" Alexandra asks.

"Of course. I know you well enough to know you wouldn't do a thing like that."

Their lunch is interrupted by a knock on the door.

They exchange questioning looks, then, Alexandra jumps up from the table, grabs her plate, and runs into the bedroom.

"Hang on one minute," Tom shouts out, "I'll be right there."

He dumps his plate and goes to answer the door. It is two uniformed officers.

"Sorry to bother you, Mr. Bouchard. I'm Officer Wallace and this is Officer Penney. We need to get into Miss Dumont's apartment again."

"Of course, just let me get the key," he says, "and I'll walk up with you."

"Have you heard anything from Miss Dumont?" Officer Wallace asks as they are walking up the stairs.

"Excuse me?" Tom answers. "Do you mean have I contacted her through a séance or something? Sorry, I don't believe in that nonsense."

"No, I mean have you spoken to her? Has she called you?"

"I'm sorry. I'm lost. Alexandra is…she's dead, isn't she?"

"Actually sir, we believe she is still alive," the officer replies.

Tom reaches out and grabs the railing. "I hope this is a convincing performance," he thinks.

"Sorry. Of course, you didn't know. Are you all right?"

Tom nods, pulls out his handkerchief, wipes his forehead and asks the detective, "How do you know she's alive? Have you seen her?"

"No, but we received a tip from an unknown caller. This caller stated Dumont is still alive and that she and her boss were lovers and planned the Judge's murder together," the detective says, carefully watching Tom's reaction.

He doesn't mention the arrest of Caitlin or her side of the story.

"Really? Wow. That's some tale," Tom says. "Do you think it's true?"

"Don't know, but, we're hoping we can turn up something in her apartment that will help us figure it out."

"Well, I'll leave you gentlemen to your job. Just drop the key off when you're done here." Tom turns and walks back down the stairs.

Waiting anxiously to learn what has happened, Alexandra hears Tom return. She waits for him to open the bedroom door, in case he is not alone.

He knocks and she calls to him to come in.

"So what's up? What did they want?" she asks.

"Well, they are not convinced you committed suicide," he answers, sounding a little short.

"What was the story Caitlin came up with?" she asks.

"It wasn't Caitlin. It was an anonymous caller who told them you were still alive and that you and Caitlin were lovers. Is it true?"

"It's true she approached me when I first began working for her. She is a very beautiful woman and I was her employee. It was difficult to refuse her, but, I did. She was fine with it."

"I see. Did you call Jake last night?"

"What? No, I didn't," she answers angrily. "Look, maybe I better leave. As soon as the cops are gone, I'll get out of your hair."

Tom looks crestfallen. He quickly apologizes for doubting her and begs her not to leave.

"I'll think about it," Alexandra says, "I'd just like to be alone for a while."

"Take all the time you need," he says.

As soon as Tom is out of the room, Alexandra gathers her few belongings and leaves the apartment through the back door. There is no one in the alley as she makes her way to the side street next to the building. She heads for her old home at the convent.

The police knock on the door 45 minutes later to return the key.

"Thanks, Mr. Bouchard."

Tom takes the key and says "thank you" to the detective. He waits a few minutes, then, knocks on the bedroom door. There's no answer. He opens the door to an empty room.

CHAPTER 9

Sitting in the holding cell, Caitlin is struggling to keep control. The family lawyer, who had some harsh words for the local police, promised to have her out before dinner time.

They had fingerprinted her, photographed her, taken her belongings, placed them in a plastic bag and escorted her to the cell.

Waiting is torture. Her mind keeps going back to her time with Jake. Her body is craving his touch. She feels as if she is in the throes of a horrible bout of withdrawal; shivering, crying, aching all over.

Hearing someone approaching her cell, she gets up. She sees her lawyer walking with the police officer. It's the last thing she sees. The entity in possession of her body departs. She begins convulsing violently as her brain is wiped clean leaving her an empty shell.

By the time the officer and the lawyer reach the cell, Caitlin is collapsed on the floor in a vegetative state.

The officer hurriedly unlocks and opens the cell door. The lawyer kneels down next to Caitlin and tries to rouse her, but, gets no response.

"Call an ambulance. What have you done to her?" he demands to know.

"Nothing, sir. We didn't do anything. It was just a routine booking. I swear she was fine when I brought her here."

None of this matters to Caitlin. She is in a place beyond reach.

CHAPTER 10

Alexandra hears the news when she stops to grab a cup of coffee.

"Prominent businesswoman, Caitlin Jensen, wife of the late Judge Harley Jensen, was arrested earlier today for the murder of her husband.

"Sources inside the police department say she is accused of taking part in a plot with her former employee, Alexandra Dumont, to murder Jensen's husband and flee the country with his money.

"When her lawyer arrived at the jail to speak with his client, he found her on the floor of her cell, unresponsive. She was transported to Tulane Medical Center and put on life support. The doctor in charge of her case, Dr. Jerry Sanford, told us she is in stable condition but could not provide us with any further details.

"Jensen had originally told police Dumont phoned her the night of the murder and lured her out of the house. She then claimed Dumont went to the house and murdered Judge Jensen, then committed suicide.

"Now police suspect Dumont and Jensen planned the murder together but believe Jensen ultimately committed the murder alone, planning to take all of the money and flee the country. Dumont is still at large and is wanted for questioning. Anyone with information related to the crime or Dumont's whereabouts is asked to call 1-800-TIP-LINE."

Dazed and confused by the news, Alexandra decides to occupy her mind trying to piece together the puzzle her life has become.

"I'm certain Caitlin and Jake are having an affair; one that may have started the night we went to Caitlin's anniversary party. I don't know whose idea it was to bump off the Judge but my bet is, Caitlin's. She seemed drawn to Jake from the get-go. She only married the Judge for his money and it was common knowledge she had not been faithful.

"I should have recognized what was happening between the two of them. The way they avoided each other whenever we were all together; how she didn't like it when I complained about him; how she flushed when I talked about our sex life; all the signs were there.

"Damn! How could I have been so stupid?"

The honking horn jolts her back to the present and she sees she has crossed at a green light. She jumps back and waves at the driver who had nearly hit her. He gives her the finger and shakes his head.

"Nice. So, where was I? The two of them decide to murder the Judge and pin it on me. They get the Judge's money and everything is rosy. So why keep me alive? Why not just eliminate me, tie up the loose end?"

She wonders if Jake is responsible for Caitlin's arrest.

"I guess that makes sense. He let her think he was going along with the plan but all the time, he had his own agenda. But why, why throw away the chance to have the money and Caitlin? It can't be because he really loves me or he would never have slept with her in the first place. Would he?"

CHAPTER 11

Killing time in his office, Jake is interrupted by his assistant. "The police are here. They would like to have a word with you."

"Send them in, Aaron," he says.

He stands and reaches out to shake Detective Thibodeaux's hand. "Good morning. What can I do for you gentlemen today?"

Sitting down across from Jake, the detective says, "We'd like to go over your story again."

"Certainly. Which part of my so-called story would you like to hear?" Jake asks.

"My apologies. I didn't mean to make it sound as if what you told us was a story and not the facts. Why don't you start with the day of the murder?"

"All right; I arrived at Alexandra's apartment about 5 pm. We talked about going to see the new movie, *Darker Demons*. I didn't have any interest, but, Alex likes...liked ghost stories."

"If I may interrupt, how long were you and Miss Dumont dating?"

"About six months. May I continue?" Jake asks.

"Of course...a little over six months you say? And you never suspected she was sleeping with her boss?" Detective Thibodeaux asks.

"I'm sorry. Did you just say Alexandra had been having an affair with Caitlin? You must be mistaken. Where did you hear this?"

"We received an anonymous phone call last night. The caller claimed Dumont and her boss were lovers," the detective tells him. "We think it is possible Jensen and Dumont plotted the murder together." the detective says. "We stopped by Mrs. Jensen's this morning."

"Stopped by? You make it sound as if you were paying a social call," Jake observes.

"No sir, we certainly weren't doing that."

"And when you stopped by, did you ask her about this supposed sexual relationship with Alexandra?" Jake wants to know.

"We did. She denied it. In fact, Mrs. Jensen insinuated you and she were having an affair."

"Really? I wonder why she would make such an absurd claim," Jake says.

"It's not true then?" the detective asks.

"It is most definitely not true," Jake replies.

"We have Jensen in custody. We found the murder weapon stashed in her office. Unfortunately, she suffered a seizure while being held. She's in the hospital," the detective tells Jake.

"That is unfortunate. Shall I continue?" Jake asks, not registering any emotion at the news of Caitlin's arrest.

"Yes...yes, please continue."

"As I was saying, we had talked about seeing the movie but Alex said she wasn't feeling well. She asked if I would mind staying in. I told her that was fine with me. We decided to order Chinese and just watch a film at home."

"What's the name of the restaurant you ordered from?" the detective asks.

"It was Chopsticks House. They delivered the food around six."

Detective Thibodeaux makes a note of this information.

"After we ate, Alex said her headache was worse and asked if I would mind just taking off."

"Was she prone to headaches?" asks the detective.

"Yes, she frequently had migraines. She had a prescription for them," Jake answers.

"Do you know her doctor's name?"

"No but I'm sure it's on the bottle," Jake says.

"Did you see her take the medicine before you left her?"

"No, I did not."

"And what time was that? What time did you leave?"

"I left at 7 pm. The news was just ending as I closed the door behind me."

Jake continues to fill in the details of the remainder of his night. He tells the detective he went home, had a couple of drinks and fell asleep in front of the television. He awakened to see his girlfriend's face on the news.

"You must have been pretty upset," Detective Thibodeaux says. It is more of a question than a statement.

"Yes, detective," Jake replies, "I left my girlfriend thinking I would see her the next day and instead, heard she had disappeared after murdering her best friend's husband. You can say I was 'pretty upset.' I would say I was devastated."

"Were you expecting to marry Miss Dumont?"

"We never discussed it but I think we had both expected our relationship to go that way," Jake replies.

"All right. Well, I think that's it for now. We'll let you know if we have any further questions."

Jake only nods his head, thinking, "You won't get anything else from me, you idiot."

CHAPTER 12

Summer hangs over the city; already steamy at 10 am. The moisture-laden air blurs the edges of the buildings. Ghost-like ripples of heat rise from the sidewalk.

Alexandra sees the familiar sign for Dauphine Street. Ringing the bell at the convent gate, she is suddenly afraid the residents will turn her away. She hasn't been in contact with anyone here for at least two years. Relief washes over her as she sees a familiar face.

"Rosslyn, it's me; it's Alexandra," she says reaching up self-consciously and tousling her short hair.

"Oh, Alex, it's wonderful to see you! I didn't recognize you! Please come in, come in," Rosslyn says opening the door and reaching out to embrace her old friend.

Overwhelmed by the warmth of the welcome and her exhaustion, Alexandra can barely stand.

"Please, I need to sit down. I…I've been through a great deal these past few days," she says.

Guiding Alexandra to a chair, Rosslyn leaves to fetch a cold drink.

"Here, have some lemonade. If I remember correctly, it was your favorite," Rosslyn says.

"Still is! This tastes wonderful," Alexandra says, gulping down the icy, sweet beverage.

"So, what has finally brought you back to us? I have a feeling this isn't just a friendly visit."

Guilt and gratitude are reflected in her features as she recounts recent events. When she has finished, Rosslyn asks, "What can we do to help?"

Shrugging her shoulders, she tells her friend, "I just felt compelled to come here. I guess I didn't know where else to go. It seems like a natural thing to want to go home when your life is coming apart."

"Of course it is, perfectly natural. You know you are always welcome here, no matter how long you stay away," Rosslyn says, trying to sound stern.

Alexandra apologizes for neglecting her surrogate family.

"I understand. Life gets complicated," Rosslyn replies.

Rosslyn leads Alexandra to a room on the second floor of the building. The space overlooks a small courtyard where the jasmine is in full bloom. Alexandra opens the window and takes in the aroma of her favorite flowers, the street sounds of the Quarter, the morning light filtering through the thick air.

Unable to remember why she was once so desperate to leave this place, she turns and tells Rosslyn, "Thank you." Rosslyn gives her a parting hug.

"Get some rest now. I will let Claire know you are here. Will you be joining us for lunch?"

"Yes, I would love that," Alexandra replies.

The instant Rosslyn is gone Alexandra collapses on the bed and immediately falls asleep.

Rosslyn rushes to Claire's office to tell her, "She's here."

CHAPTER 13

Alexandra awakens. Momentarily confused, she searches the room for anything familiar. Heart pounding, she gets up and walks to the window. Realizing with relief she is back in the convent, she shakes her head and smiles.

"A little shell-shocked, aren't we?" she asks herself. She heads down the hall to the bathroom. The shower is on the cool side, triggering memories of her past.

"This place never did have decent hot water. You would think they'd have gotten it fixed by now," she grumbles to herself.

Gazing in the mirror she barely recognizes the gaunt woman with the short maize-colored hair.

"We have come a long way baby. Now, where do we go from here?"

A knock on the door interrupts her musing.

"Alexandra? Are you in there? We are ready to sit down to lunch," Rosslyn tells her, through the door.

"Yes, Rossy. I'll be down in a few minutes."

Giggling, her friend replies, "No one has called me that since you left."

She finishes dressing. Squaring her shoulders, she prepares herself for what is coming; each step down to the dining room takes her farther back in time until she is once again a child.

Claire looks up when Alexandra enters the dining room. Indicating the chair beside her, she says, "Come and sit by me."

Doing as Claire instructs, Alexandra responds, "Thank you for allowing me to stay Claire. I didn't know where else to go."

"You are always welcome. We'll talk after lunch."

Alexandra has no intention of remaining at the convent but answers, "All right. I look forward to catching up."

A sidelong glance lets Alexandra know her fib has been instantly detected.

When lunch is finished, Claire reaches out and takes Alexandra's hand. There is no way for her to politely escape. She follows Claire to her office.

Sitting across from the still-youthful-looking woman she has known all her life, Alexandra is nervous as a guilty child about to be scolded. Compulsively tapping the arm of the chair, she waits for Claire to begin.

"We have heard the stories on the news; stories of murder and adultery. Are they true?"

"No. I was not having an affair with Caitlin's husband, nor with Caitlin, and I did not kill the Judge," Alexandra tells her.

"Can you tell me exactly what happened?" Claire asks.

"I can tell you what I remember."

Alexandra recounts the events leading up to her arrival at the convent gate. When she is finished, Claire asks to hear more about Jake.

"I'm not sure what you want to know. He is handsome, probably the best-looking man I have ever known. It was strange though, sometimes when I would mention to someone how I loved his brown eyes, or his thick, wavy hair, they would look puzzled; almost as if the man I was describing was not the one they were seeing.

"We met at the library. I was doing some research for a work project and he asked me to help him find some books on New Orleans history; Marie Laveau in particular. I knew he didn't need my help, he was flirting and that was fine with me.

"We started dating and he was amazing; very caring and smart and the sex was incredible…sorry, I mean…"

"Alexandra, you know that sort of talk isn't a problem here."

"I know it's just that it still embarrasses me to talk about it. I've never felt so, I don't know, addicted to someone."

"I was afraid of that," she tells Alexandra. "It's possible your Jake is not human. I would need more information to be sure, however, he sounds like one of the demonkind. They are extremely attractive and almost impossible to resist once in your blood. In fact, if I am correct, I might even know his name; his real name."

"Jake…a demon? Do such things really exist?" she asks.

"That question seems odd coming from someone who was raised by her fellow witches, and whose father is a powerful warlock," Claire responds. "Why would you question the existence of demons?"

"I would prefer it if you did not mention my father. He never even cared enough about me to come and visit me," Alexandra says.

Shaking her head as if to scold Alexandra, Claire says, "That isn't true. He visited you often when you were very young. As you got older he found it difficult. You greatly resemble your mother."

Angrily, Alexandra replies, "He found it difficult? I lost my mother and my father deserted me. Am I supposed to feel sorry for him?"

Claire tries to calm Alexandra, saying, "Of course not. I'm just trying to explain his behavior. He does love you, and I'm sure he is concerned for you, especially now."

A cloud of foreboding creeps over Alexandra as she listens to these words. "What do you mean? You mean because the police are looking for me?"

Claire shakes her head. "I think it's best if your father explains everything to you," she tells the bewildered woman sitting before her.

"All right, then tell me how to find him and I will ask him," she says.

Again, Claire shakes her head. "I wish I could but it's better if he contacts you. I believe he will find you when he's ready."

CHAPTER 14

Leaving the convent after her conversation with Claire, Alexandra feels more lost than ever. Was it possible Claire had told her the truth? Was Jake a demon? And then all that talk about her father...

"Just wait and your father will find you," was not what she wanted to hear.

Now she is back on the familiar streets of the Vieux Carre´; wandering aimlessly, unsure what she is looking for. Not paying attention to where she is going, she bumps into a tall man apparently stationed in the middle of the sidewalk.

Startled she looks up and sees a familiar face. "Tom? What the...what are you doing here?" she asks, gazing at him as if he is an apparition.

"I told you I would help you. I like to keep my promises."

"I'm sorry, sorry about running out on you. I felt I didn't have a choice," she explains.

"I understand. I should never have questioned you like I did. I know you wouldn't have called Jake, not after what happened. I grabbed some more of your things before I left and put them in my apartment," he tells her.

"Thanks," she says. "I don't know how safe it is for me to go back there. Maybe you could bring the clothes to the convent, or something...I don't know," she replies.

Tom asks Alexandra what she is planning and what he can do to help. Her only answer is a shrug of the shoulders.

"I don't have a plan, I'm afraid."

Suggesting they start by visiting the library, he takes her hand and heads in that direction.

"Why the library?" she asks.

"I thought we could look up some family histories; see if there is any connection between Jake's family and yours, or Caitlin's," he explains. "Maybe figure out why they did this to you."

"I'm pretty sure there are no connections. They did this because they are having an affair. Then for some reason, Jake couldn't bring himself to kill me, which, I believe, had been the original plan," she tells him.

Tom presses her to tell him why she is so sure of this, but, Alexandra refuses, saying only her family history is not something she wants to examine.

Reluctant to let the idea go, he keeps pressing for details until she finally lashes out at him.

"Just let it go! We're not looking into my family. Stop badgering me!" she screams at him, causing passersby to cast wary looks in their direction.

"Geez, relax. I didn't know it was such a touchy subject," Tom tells her.

Pulling her hand out of his grasp, she asks him to leave her alone. "Just go back home. You shouldn't have come looking for me in the first place."

"I'm sorry. Please, I just want to help," he pleads. Relenting, she tells him he may stay if he promises not to pry into her personal history. "If I ask you to leave something alone, just do it," she commands.

They start off again, this time in the direction of the river.

Alexandra is hungry and suggests they stop at the Café du Monde for some beignets.

"Not a very healthy choice," Tom says.

Rolling her eyes, she leads Tom to a table. She orders half a dozen beignets and two cafés au lait. While waiting for their order, they are joined by an unfamiliar woman.

"Who are you, and what do you think you are doing just seating yourself at our table like this?' Alexandra demands to know.

"Cher, my name wouldn't mean anything to you. I have a message. Meet me at midnight tonight in Saint Louis Cemetery," she says, looking not at Alexandra, but at Tom. Then as quickly as she had appeared she is up and gone.

Confounded, Alexandra just shakes her head. "She is probably just a con woman trying to lure unsuspecting tourists to the cemetery so she can rob them."

Tom doesn't say anything to Alexandra but his curiosity is piqued. He wonders if the strange woman had anything to do with Alexandra's ordeal. Could she have taken part in the kidnapping?

He decides to follow her orders and meet her at midnight in the cemetery.

Following their beignet stop, the two wander aimlessly through the dense, humid air.

Dreamily, Alexandra says, "It's always so hot and humid in the summer." Hearing the odd tone in her voice, Tom turns to look at her, but she is gone.

Terrified, he begins calling her name. He pushes through people lazily strolling by the river, eliciting angry stares. He can't quite get his brain to accept the reality; Alexandra has vanished, leaving nothing behind but the scent of jasmine.

CHAPTER 15

Feeling as if an ill wind has picked her up and deposited her unceremoniously on the floor, she looks up at the unfamiliar face of the man towering over her. He reaches down and offers his hand. Pushing it aside, she stands on her own.

"Who are you?" she demands to know.

"My name is Gregory," he tells her. "But, that's probably not what you meant is it?"

"I want to know who you are and why you have brought me here," she answers. She notices her surroundings are elegant and obviously expensive. Even a cursory glance around convinces her, the room is filled with priceless artifacts. Her eyes light up when they come to rest on what, to her, appears to be an original Picasso.

"I see you are an art lover. I have many valuable pieces you would undoubtedly enjoy."

"What is this, some kind of museum or gallery?" she asks, momentarily forgetting she has been kidnapped.

"No, my dear. This is simply my home."

"How can that be?" she asks. "The artwork in this room alone is worth, what…billions?"

"I would expect so," her host answers, smiling. Remembering how she came to be in the company of this strange man, she resumes her questioning. "How did I get here?"

"One of my assistants brought you," he tells her.

"I want you to answer my questions."

"I thought I did answer your question. You were brought here by one of my assistants. Is that not what you asked?" he says.

"No human could have whisked me away and delivered me here in less time than it takes to blink," Alexandra answers.

"No, that's quite true, but then, Samir is not human. He is a wind wraith," Gregory explains.

"I have never heard of such a thing," she says.

"The witches haven't done a very thorough job of educating you, have they? Allow me to elaborate. I am a warlock; an extremely powerful one much like your father."

Alexandra demands to know how Gregory is acquainted with her father, "And how do you know I was raised by the witches? I want to know who you are!"

"I told you, my name is Gregory. I have known your father for…let's just say a very long time. I knew your mother as well. As for Samir, he is a wind wraith; created when this planet was young.

"He was conjured by the earliest inhabitants of this planet. They combined the four elements, air, water, fire and earth; and created Samir. He is the only one of his kind," Gregory says.

"Do you really expect me to believe any of this? Stop telling me fairy tales and tell me why you brought me here? What do you want with me?"

Gregory replies, "Oh, they are not fairy tales Alexandra. You are the key to everything and I need you to reveal your secrets to me."

At that instant, another force takes hold of Alexandra and spirits her away. Her brain, already overloaded, shuts down and she passes out, finally reawakening outside her apartment building.

CHAPTER 16

At a loss for what to do or where to go after Alexandra's abrupt disappearance, Tom heads back to his apartment. The heat is becoming mind-melting. Imagining Alexandra everywhere, he is barely able to make it back home.

As he strides along, he is suddenly confronted by a large tabby cat. The cat stubbornly blocks his path. Exasperated, he bends down to pick it up and the cat claws at his arm leaving a scratch several inches long.

"Shit. That's all I need," he says angrily.

Opening the door to his apartment, at last, the cool air rushes to him, surrounding him, caressing him; leading him to the softness of the bed. Stripping off his damp clothes he climbs between the soothing sheets. Behind his eyelids, he sees her beckoning.

Awakening hours later, he notices there is no longer any sliver of daylight stealing through the blinds. It is 9 pm and he is still alone.

Cleaning off the dirt of the hellishly hot day and bandaging his arm, he dresses for dinner out, not knowing what else to do. Opening the door leading to the courtyard in front of the building he discovers Alexandra. His joy at seeing her is tempered by the sight of her disheveled appearance. She is sitting at one of the tables, head resting in hands.

"Alex, what happened? You look terrible."

She doesn't answer him. She just sits, staring straight ahead. Picking her up as he would a child and carrying her into the apartment, he gently places her on his bed.

Undressing her, he examines her body for injuries. She appears unhurt. There are no bruises, no discolorations.

Gently running his hands all over, he feels nothing broken.

"You are too beautiful to be real," he thinks. Caressing her breast, he sees her body respond. Kissing her neck while his fingers move between her legs, he hears her moan, jolting him back to reality.

"What's wrong with me? I can't take advantage of her like this," he says out loud.

"I'm running a nice warm bath for you," he tells Alexandra. "Everything is going to be fine. I'll take care of you."

Finally, she turns to him, acknowledging his presence. She places her hand on his cheek. "So good…you are so good to me," she says.

Tom adds some of her jasmine bath oil to the tub, hoping Alexandra will find it soothing. Picking her up again, he carries her into the bathroom.

"I don't want to try and lower you in," he says. "I'm afraid I might drop you."

"It's all right. You can put me down. I'm starting to get my strength back," she tells him.

He sets her down. Her arms reach up to him. She presses her naked body against him urging him to finish what he started. Bending down, he kisses her warm, welcoming mouth. Feeling himself sinking into her, he pulls back.

"Not now, not like this," he tells her. "Take your bath. I'll go get us something to eat," he says, rushing out of the room before he can change his mind.

Lowering herself into the waiting water, Alexandra inhales the jasmine and finally begins to unwind. She picks up the soap and begins lathering herself with slow, soothing strokes. Eyes closed, she sees Jake's face. She is lost in the fantasy when Tom returns and knocks on the door.

"Come on in and join me," she says dreamily. Tom opens the door as she opens her eyes and comes back to reality.

Embarrassed by her thoughts, she asks Tom to give her some privacy.

He sets up their dinner while Alexandra wraps herself in his robe, so large she feels like a tiny child floating inside of it. Sitting down opposite him, she is suddenly famished.

"This smells wonderful. Crawfish Etouffee is one of my favorites," she tells Tom, breaking off a piece of the crusty bread and dipping it in the rich sauce.

"I got us some beer too," he tells her, opening a couple of icy cold Abitas. "Do you think you can tell me what happened to you?" he asks.

"Just let me relax," she says. "I will tell you everything I remember in a bit, although it isn't much."

The two of them eat dinner in silence. Alexandra is still lost in her thoughts of Jake, not really able to understand how she can still have feelings for him. Tom is waiting patiently for her to open up and tell him what happened.

Finally, unable to take the silence any longer, Tom snaps, "Alexandra, please, can you just say something!"

Shaken out of her reverie, she looks across the table at him. "I'm sorry. What is it you want me to say?"

Throwing down his napkin and pushing back his chair, Tom gets up and slams out of the room. Unable or unwilling to go after him wearing only a bathrobe, Alexandra stays where she is and finishes her meal.

An unfamiliar feeling of rage is coursing through Tom's body as he explodes through the door of his apartment.

Getting into his car, he heads for Saint Louis Cemetery. "Alexandra may have thought that woman was crazy, but, I need to find out for myself," he thinks.

Tom parks the car on Dauphine Street. He is tempted by the noise of the revelers on Bourbon Street but his destination is in the opposite direction. He turns away and heads down St. Louis Street.

As he walks, the sultry air causes a heavy feeling in his chest. He thinks, "I feel like I am trying to breathe underwater."

Sounds are muffled. Buildings washed in watercolor gray fade in and out of his sight. He has no company as he approaches Basin Street and turns towards the cemetery.

There is a locked gate at the entrance, but he easily locates a fence he is able to climb over. Removing a map from his pocket, he realizes he doesn't need it. He wends his way through the maze of crypts; knowing where to go without understanding how.

"How is it I know exactly where I am going when I have never been here before?" he muses.

Arriving at the crypt allegedly containing the body of Marie Laveau, he searches for the strange woman from Café du Monde. He doesn't see her anywhere, but, when he turns around she is standing beside it.

"You startled me," he tells her.

"You need to pay attention, boy. You got to be careful. New Orleans can be a dangerous place if you ain't," she scolds him.

"I will remember that," he tells her.

"You best take me seriously. That woman you're in love with is in danger, and you got to protect her. Can't do that if you ain't paying attention!"

Tom is feeling the stirrings of his previous anger when he asks, "What do you know about her? What kind of danger is she in?"

"Now you just settle down and I tell you. Your lady, she don't understand who she is. She thinks this here lady whose name is on the grave, this Marie Laveau, is her great-great-great-great grandmother. She's wrong. Marie is her mother and her name ain't Marie, it's Lorelei! Alexandra's mama only jes' died 32 years ago! There's nobody in this grave," the woman proclaims extending her arm and pointing to the crypt with a flourish.

Barely containing his fury, he says, "Alexandra was right. You're just some crazy woman out to fleece people." He turns around to leave but she grabs his arm.

"Now you listen to me, boy. I ain't crazy. I'm telling you the honest truth. You find a man named Lucien de la Terre and you ask him about your lady."

Tom wanders back to the car wondering what he will tell Alexandra tomorrow. She wakes up briefly when he returns. He doesn't want to disturb her any further. He decides to sleep on the couch. That is how they spend the remainder of the night.

CHAPTER 17

The morning after Detective Thibodeaux's visit,
Jake is packed and ready to remove his belongings from
the apartment he and Caitlin had occasionally shared
and return them to his house on Royal Street. There is
still one loose end he needs to tie up.

Heading for the hospital he feels a faint memory of
desire for the woman he is about to dispatch. He
remembers her as a skilled partner; easily manipulated,
at least in the beginning. She had been more than willing
to engage in some truly depraved acts.

He had not anticipated the affair with Caitlin.
Initially, he had only wanted to meet Alexandra. Rumors
in New Orleans were rampant that Lucien de la Terre's
daughter had finally reached sexual maturity. His
curiosity about the gorgeous Alexandra was irresistible.

Quickly discovering the rumors were true, Jake had
enthusiastically seduced her. He hadn't expected the
involvement to last; they never did. But, inexplicably,
one month became two, then six, and still, they were
together.

Jake's relationship with Caitlin, on the other hand,
was only an entertaining diversion; at least for him. She
had wanted him from their first contact. He found her
attractive and responded by initiating the affair.
Alexandra never suspected her boyfriend and best friend
were feeding her a constant stream of lies.

Gradually over the course of their relationship,
Caitlin's personality had changed. Her sexual appetites
became so twisted even Jake was disturbed by them.
There was a cruel edge to everything she did.

He was unable to pinpoint the exact moment he realized she had become a different person. He felt it began shortly after an incident which occurred outside her office one afternoon.

As she told it, she was walking down the steps when a huge white cat planted itself in her path. She had tried to walk around it, but the creature kept darting from side to side, preventing her escape. Finally, it reached up and clawed her leg, leaving a nasty scratch. After that, it had bounded down the steps and disappeared. Jake wondered if it had infected her with some virus which altered her behavior.

It wasn't long after that she approached him with the plan. Suggesting they would be better off with the Judge no longer in the picture, she explained her idea. She would shoot her husband and make it look as if Alexandra had committed the crime.

"I'll tell the police she and the Judge were having an affair but he refused to divorce me, so she murdered him," she said.

Then, once the Judge was dead, the two of them would take his money and move far away from New Orleans.

He asked what they would do about Alexandra. "Kill her of course," she answered, laughing.

"We'll make it look like a suicide."

Hoping to buy some time, Jake presented her with an alternative scenario. He suggested they kidnap Alexandra and pump her full of drugs, "Convince her she is losing her mind," he told her. "We can use the brain wave altering chip I invented to control her visions.

"Then, we tell the police she threatened to kill herself so they won't be looking for her, at least they won't be looking for a live Alexandra. When she can't tell what's real and what isn't, you call the police and say she is still alive and she is coming after you and she has a gun. We'll stage it to look as if you shot her in self-defense."

He finally convinced her it was the smartest way to handle it and Caitlin had carried out her part of the plan. Framing Caitlin for the murder had been his plan all along.

He enters her room unseen and leans over her. He can't sense any spirit in the once vibrant body. Placing his mouth over hers, he sucks out what little life remains. "Sorry darling, but, I'm sure you understand it's nothing personal."

As the monitor begins to screech, indicating Caitlin's death, Jake disappears.

CHAPTER 18

Awakening to an empty apartment, Alexandra finds a note on the pillow next to her head. Tom has gone to get them both some coffee and pick up a copy of the *Times-Picayune*. She heads to the bathroom to get dressed.

Her mind is a maze she is having trouble navigating. Scenes of a past life, that seems to belong to someone else, interfere with the present reality. Remembering her visit with Gregory, she wonders what he meant by "you are the key." She knows of no connection between them, yet he claimed to know both of her parents. She hears Tom return and throws on the robe to go out and greet him.

He is beginning to look like she feels. Huge circles surround his eyes; his usually pale skin is almost ashen. Even his body looks different; smaller and less sturdy.

"Hey, good morning. You look terrible. Are you doing all right?" she asks.

"Under the circumstances, yes, I am doing all right. How are you?" he answers, not smiling.

"Confused and tired."

He hands her a coffee and sits down at the small, antique table. "Are you ready to tell me what happened yesterday?" he asks.

Sitting down opposite him, she says, "I will tell you what I remember. Some of it is pretty hard to believe."

"Alexandra, after the week I have had, I will believe almost anything," he says.

Studying his face for any trace of the Tom she used to know and finding none, she begins her story. She tells him about Gregory; how he had claimed to be a warlock almost as old as civilization itself.

"The one room I was in had artifacts worth millions, and he implied the rest of the house was the same. He may be lying about how old he is but, at the very least, he is incredibly wealthy," she says.

She goes on to recount the tale Claire had told her of the alleged demon, Jake. Tom seems very willing to believe this part of the story.

She tells him the creature that had grabbed her from the street was what Gregory termed a wind wraith. "His name is Samir," she says.

"So how did you end up back here?" he asks.

"I don't know. One minute I was in his house, the next I was sitting in the courtyard outside the apartment. I don't know where I was or what happened in between," she tells him, afraid he is going to lose his temper again.

Instead, he reaches out and takes her hand. "I have something I need to tell you," he says.

Suddenly terrified he is going to send her away, she tells him to go ahead.

"I went to the cemetery last night. The woman from the Café du Monde was there."

Alexandra tries to interrupt but Tom puts his fingers over her mouth.

"Please, just wait until I am done," he says.

She nods her head, and he continues. "I made my way to Marie Laveau's tomb. I felt as if some force was moving me, guiding me. I didn't see her at first but then she appeared suddenly; I want to say she materialized. She told me I need to protect you, however, she didn't say from what. And…she said you are the daughter of

Marie Laveau, only that isn't her real name. She said her real name is Lorelei."

Stunned by this piece of information, Alexandra shakes her head. "It can't be true."

"So warlocks, demons, and wind wraiths; those things you can believe in. But not the fact you are the daughter of Marie Laveau?"

"Tom, it's absurd. She died over 125 years ago. That would mean I am over 125 years old. Does that make sense?" she asks.

"According to her, the grave of Marie Laveau is empty. Your mother died 32 years ago, just as you were told, but she had once been known as Marie Laveau."

"I can't digest all of this on an empty stomach," Alexandra says.

"Then why don't you get dressed and we can go get some breakfast?"

"Do you think that's safe?" she asks. "My picture is plastered everywhere, all over the internet and the TV. We've been lucky so far but, the police are probably watching you. In fact, I'm surprised they didn't find me in the courtyard yesterday. They could come knocking on the door at any time."

Acknowledging Alexandra is right, he tells her about a hidden room in the basement of the apartment building.

"I discovered it by accident one day when I was cleaning. I don't know what it was used for; don't know if I want to, but I fixed it up and it's pretty comfortable," he informs her. "I'll take you there and then get us something to eat and bring it down to you. You'll be completely safe there even if the police come looking for you."

Not really relishing the idea of being locked in the basement, Alexandra reluctantly agrees, saying, "I guess it will be fine as long as it's just for a few minutes."

Leading her down the rickety stairs, Tom is careful to clear the cobwebs hanging from the ceiling. He stomps his feet to frighten away any mice that might be scavenging for crumbs.

"It's over here," he tells her, moving a mirror to expose the door to the hidden room.

Shivering at the sight of it, she walks over and waits while Tom puts his key in the rusty lock. The door opens to a small room, almost a closet. A bed and a chest of drawers are the only furnishings. The ancient lamp on the chest throws little light, leaving the corners of the room in shadow.

"Wow, I don't like the feel of this at all," she tells Tom.

"It's temporary, and it's safe. You'll be fine here," he assures her. "I'm just going to run out and get us something to eat. I'll be back before you know it."

Tom's departure, accompanied by the sound of the key turning in the lock once again, sends a cloud of despair over Alexandra.

Pulling her cell phone out of her pocket, she is not surprised to see there are no bars. Jake's smiling face is there, however. She runs her fingers over the screen, aching to feel his skin. Her tears are falling on the glass making it look as though Jake is crying.

"Do demons cry?" she wonders.

Increasingly agitated and afraid as the minutes drag by, Alexandra begins pacing back and forth in the tiny room. Not normally claustrophobic, the dense air and fetid atmosphere of the space are causing her to feel suffocated. Checking her phone again to see how long Tom has been absent, she sees it has been over an hour.

"It shouldn't take such a long time for him to get us some breakfast," she thinks.

The fear that he has left her to die in the room nobody knows of grips her insides; twists them until she doubles over in pain. When she opens her eyes again, she is in Tom's kitchen.

At that instant, the door opens and Tom comes in carrying their breakfast. Seeing her agitated state he asks, "What's wrong? What the hell happened?"

"What? Are you insane?" she screams. "You put me in that horrible room in the basement and then left me there. You told me you were going to get us something to eat then you locked me in. That was over an hour ago."

"Alexandra, you just saw me walk through the door," he says.

"Yes, I did, but you came home a little while ago. We talked about last night. You told me you had gone to the cemetery," she says.

Startled, he answers, "I did go there but, how…I don't understand what's happening. I swear to you we did not have that conversation and I did not put you in that room," he insists. "And, if you were locked in, how did you get out?"

CHAPTER 19

Rosslyn is clearing up the breakfast dishes when Claire approaches her.

"Rosslyn, please come with me. I think we need to talk about Alexandra," Claire says.

Rosslyn follows her to the courtyard in the center of the convent. They seat themselves on a bench beneath the ancient oak; planted by the first of their order

"I am afraid for her," Claire begins. "She has never been told the full story of her birth or her parents. She is not equipped to deal with what may be coming."

Rosslyn agrees. "Maybe it's time for her to learn the truth in order to protect herself."

"Is she strong enough?" Claire asks.

Alexandra's old friend looks concerned when she answers, "I truly don't know, but, I'm afraid it's time to find out."

Tom is still waiting for an explanation when Alexandra's phone rings. She holds up her hand to Tom, "It's Rosslyn, it's all right."

She walks outside with the phone to her ear, nodding as she listens to Rosslyn. Finishing the call, she turns to Tom.

"She and Claire want me to come to the convent. They need to talk to me about something. I think I should go alone," she tells him.

"Why do you still call it a convent?" he asks somewhat angrily.

"That's how I've always referred to it," she answers. "What would you like me to call it?"

"Call it what it is, a coven," he says, turning his back on Alexandra.

"How do you know that? I've never told you what they are," Alexandra asks.

"You mean what they are, and what you are?" Tom answers walking back into the apartment and slamming the door.

Rosslyn is by the gate when Alexandra arrives. She gives her friend a reassuring hug, something which only serves to make Alexandra more apprehensive.

They walk in silence. Claire is waiting for them in the courtyard. The air is slightly cooler in the shade of the giant oak but it still clings to Alexandra's skin and settles heavily in her lungs. The jasmine scent is absent here. The air is dominated by the citrusy smell of lemons, emanating from the trees planted in each corner.

"Sit down Alexandra, and don't look so terrified. Things are going to be all right," Claire says.

Sinking into the cushioned chair opposite Claire, Alexandra asks, "Are they?"

Claire tries to summon a smile. "Of course they are," she says.

Claire begins by asking how much of her childhood Alexandra can recall. She responds most of her memories are faint; thin wisps of moments that disappear when she tries to focus on them.

"Mostly I remember smells and sounds; the scent of jasmine; the sound of horses walking on the cobblestones. I remember walking through the market; all the people, the bright colors, the music."

"Do you remember much about your father?" Claire asks.

"Why are you asking questions about my father again? I don't remember anything about him from my childhood," Alexandra answers.

"As I told you before, he visited regularly when you were young. He told you stories about your mother. Don't you have any recollection of that?" Claire prods her.

Feeling her frustration mounting, Alexandra says she does not remember. She asks what it is Claire wants to tell her.

"I need to find a way to clear my name, I can't spend all day sitting around doing nothing," she says.

Hesitantly, Claire tells her the true identity of her mother. "Marie Laveau was not your great-great-great-great-grandmother, Alex, she was your mother."

Shaking her head, she refuses to believe the news. "You are the second person to tell me that and I still don't believe it."

Startled, Claire tells her, "It's true, whether you believe it or not."

Rising from her chair, Alexandra tells them she has heard enough. She is leaving.

They don't attempt to stop her, but, ask her to please think about what she has learned.

"When you understand, come back, and we'll talk," Rosslyn tells her, hoping it will happen sooner rather than later.

CHAPTER 20

Tom fetches a beer from the previous night out of the refrigerator and sits down at the wrought iron kitchen table. His thoughts are only of Alexandra. He is worried about what the witches are telling her.

The worry is escalating to panic when he hears someone knocking on the side door. Alexandra enters wearing an expression of anger tinged with fear. He reaches out his arms but she ignores them and sits down opposite him.

Holding up a hand to forestall any questions, she tells him, "I am very confused right now; very upset. I don't think I can take the third degree."

He doesn't reply, just opens another beer and hands it to her. Tom turns on the TV and tunes it to the local news. There are the usual stories about politics and mayhem, then…

"Caitlin Jensen, the widow of Judge Harley Jensen, died early this morning. The cause of death has not been released.

"In another bizarre twist to this already strange story, we have learned that Jensen confessed to single-handedly murdering her husband. The confession came in the form of a letter mailed to police shortly before Jensen's arrest.

"Handwriting experts have confirmed the letter was written by Jensen. In it, she claims full responsibility for her husband's murder. 'I acted alone out of jealousy and anger. Alexandra had nothing to do with the murder of my husband. They were never involved in an affair. I was. I am in love with another man and his rejection of me was too much. I thought once my husband was gone

*and I was free, he would come around but... I can't live
like this. I can't go on...'*

"The note continues, explaining how Jensen had
kidnapped Dumont and kept her prisoner in an
abandoned warehouse with the aid of two unnamed
accomplices. It becomes more rambling and incoherent
before finally ending with an apology to Dumont.

"Authorities believe Jensen wrote the note, mailed it
then took an overdose of medication prescribed for
depression before police arrived at her house
Wednesday morning. An autopsy performed on Jensen
confirmed massive amounts of the drug were present in
her body at the time of her death.

"Detective Thibodeaux, the officer in charge of the
investigation, confirmed all evidence pointed to Jensen
acting alone. When he was asked why Jensen had not
simply confessed when she was questioned, he
answered, 'Who knows? She was a seriously disturbed
woman who had thrown everything away for a man who
didn't want her.'

"Authorities are still searching for Dumont's body,
however, they now believe she is alive and possibly in
hiding. They have dropped all charges. According to
Detective Thibodeaux, 'Our investigation is closed and
Miss Dumont has been exonerated. If she would like to
come to the station and tell us her version of events, just
to wrap this whole thing up, we would be happy to speak
with her.'"

Alexandra is stunned by the announcement.

"Jake had nothing to do with it after all," she says,
joyfully.

"That's all you can think of, Jake? This is crazy. Don't you realize Jake is the man she talks about in the letter? You are still hooked on him, aren't you?"

Wishing she could give Tom a different answer, she tells him, "I don't know, maybe I am. I'm sorry."

"How can you just forget everything that happened? Think about it. How did Caitlin manage to kidnap you and hold you in that hospital if Jake wasn't helping her? How did she manage to control your mind and create those hallucinations? Don't you see this is some kind of game he's playing?"

"I'm sorry Tom, but, I know there is some explanation for everything that happened."

Disgusted and speechless, Tom walks out without even bothering to close the door.

Once Tom has left, Alexandra attempts to write a note of apology. Deciding it will only make matters worse she tears it up. Instead, she simply writes "farewell" on a sheet of stationery.

"I do hope you fare well," she thinks. "You deserve to be happy."

She opens the door to Tom's bedroom and locates the ring holding the key to her apartment.

Stopping in the doorway, she is overcome by sadness. Thinking she might be making a mistake, she almost turns around. Then her mind is filled with images of Jake and she walks away.

Still seething, Tom arrives at the convent gate. He rings the bell and Rosslyn appears.

Hesitant to open the gate to a stranger, Rosslyn asks what he wants. He says he is a friend of Alexandra's and he would like to come in and talk to them about her.

"I'm sorry but we don't really allow any visitors," she tells him.

Begging her to reconsider, Tom explains that he believes Alexandra is in danger. "I know she has enemies," he says. "I just want to help."

Finally relenting, Rosslyn opens the gate and leads him to Claire's office.

CHAPTER 21

Alexandra's sense of relief leaves her breathless. It has only been a few days since the beginning of her ordeal, yet she feels a lifetime older. Her joy at the news briefly replaces her consternation over the conversation with Claire.

Once back in her own apartment, Alexandra picks up the phone. She is about to call Jake when the truth crashes down on her; Tom was right. Caitlin could not have done it alone.

Everything she imagined happening between Caitlin and Jake undoubtedly had happened. Claire had hinted at Jake's true nature; yet, she still ached for him.

"I have to rid myself of this addiction before I lose my mind," she tells herself. "If what Claire said is true and Jake is not human, I have to stay away from him. But then, I am not human either. Maybe we belong together."

She feels her resolve beginning to weaken again and realizes she can't free herself from Jake's hold without help. Heading for the door, she tosses her phone on the bed. "At least I can stop myself from calling him," she thinks.

By the time she reaches the convent gate, she has once again convinced herself of Jake's innocence. She is about to turn around when she hears someone calling out to her.

"Alexandra, please don't walk away again. We only want to help you."

"Tom? What are you doing here? What's going on?" she asks.

Tom opens the gate and implores her to come inside, telling her, "Claire will explain everything. Please."

Reluctantly, Alexandra enters the convent grounds. The sound of the closing gate, reminiscent of the awful basement room, makes her feel trapped once again.

Turning around, she says, "No, I can't do this. I need to go now."

Tom reaches out and takes her hand, gently pulling her towards the conversation she needs to have with Claire. Each step is a struggle; desire causing her feet to falter on the path but she keeps following Tom.

CHAPTER 22

Approaching his master, Aaron asks if he should make dinner reservations. "It's almost 7:30," he says.

"Thank you for the time update, Aaron. Yes, contact Cassandra and tell her I require a companion for the evening then make a reservation for us at Brennan's."

Aaron follows his master's instructions and returns to inform Jake, Cassandra will be waiting at the restaurant. "Is there anything else?" he asks.

Jake tells him he is free to go and prowl the streets, "I won't be requiring your services anymore tonight."

Walking the few blocks to the restaurant, Jake's thoughts return to Alexandra. He was pleased to learn his note to the police had not been detected as a forgery. The last loose end had been neatly tied up.

He had expected Alexandra to call as soon as the news came out that the charges had been dropped. She had not. Maybe she had pieced everything together and realized he had been Caitlin's accomplice and lover. Still, he feels he deserves an opportunity to explain his side.

The air around him crackles with angry flashes of red. People cross the street to escape the heat pouring off him. They notice a strange smell as he passes; a scent akin to rotten eggs.

Cassandra is waiting for him in front of Brennan's. He grabs her with such force her head snaps back with an audible crack. His lips find her neck leaving a red mark that will take months to disappear.

"Nice to see you too Jake," she says.

"Let's skip the dinner," he snarls, "I find I have no appetite for the food they serve here."

Grabbing Cassandra's arm, Jake forcefully guides her back to the house on Royal Street. Slamming the door behind them, he pulls her body close. She pushes away, telling him to be patient, they have all night.

Suddenly, Jake's desire rushes from his body leaving him cold and shaken. He turns on Cassandra, ordering her to leave.

She moves towards him, touches his cheek. "What's the matter, Jake? Afraid you're not enough of a demon to satisfy a real woman?" she taunts.

Enraged, he grabs her and forces her to the floor. He tears her clothes away and uses his teeth to gently pierce her naked flesh; tiny bites meant to arouse. Cassandra is groaning, begging him not to stop. His bites grow increasingly violent. His teeth are ripping her flesh, making terrible wounds.

Terrified now, she tries to force him away, begging him to stop. Barely able to control himself, he pulls away from Cassandra.

Trembling with rage, he tells Cassandra to go to the upstairs bedroom and put some clothes on. "Then get out before I kill you," he says.

Cassandra does as she is told and gets dressed. Storming out the door, she mocks him asking, "Where is your beloved witch? Has she lost interest in her pet demon?"

Springing after her, Jake reaches the door one second too late. Cassandra is gone, racing down the street. He lets her go.

CHAPTER 23

The heat of the day has been broken by a series of thunderstorms leaving the air in the courtyard sharp, almost cool. The sun hasn't set, but the canopy of trees creates a false twilight. Candles are lit along the perimeter and on the table.

Pouring a glass of wine for each of them, Claire raises her glass and tilts it towards Alexandra. "A toast to the truth," she says.

Alexandra is filled with nervous energy. Her skin feels taut, stretched to the breaking point; her hands won't stay still. She gulps down her wine and tilts her glass towards Rosslyn wanting more.

"Please try and relax. We may be here a long time," Claire says.

Standing up, she paces like a trapped animal. She can almost feel the growl rising in her throat.

"Why does Tom have to be here?" she demands to know. "He doesn't have anything to do with this place. Really, he has little to do with me."

She hears the small grunt escape from his lips. "Perhaps it would be better if you waited in the front hall," Claire says to Tom. "There are private things we need to talk to Alexandra about."

Tom reluctantly gets up and leaves the courtyard.

"I'll sit down now, but, can we please just get this over with?"

"All right. Let me begin by saying everything we have done has been done to protect you. I know you may not believe it right now, but it is the truth."

"Why makes you think I need protecting?" Alexandra asks.

"You have enemies, possibly many. I would think your experiences of the past week would have made that clear," Claire answers.

"Well, whatever you have been doing to protect me hasn't worked very well, has it?" Alexandra says, casting an angry look at Claire.

Claire continues, "That is probably true. We have always had your best interests at heart, however."

Alexandra lets out a sigh of exasperation, "You know what they say about good intentions…"

Claire clears her throat to refocus everyone's attention. "If I may continue, your mother, Lorelei, also known as Marie Laveau…"

Claire holds up her hand as she sees Alexandra preparing to interrupt. "I know you are having trouble believing it. She was, however, your mother. We are all far older than you realize."

Standing again, Alexandra says, "Stop being so cryptic. Come to the point. Who or what are we?"

"We are beings who came here when civilization was young. In the early days, the earth was home to many incredible species. Most have now faded into legend; becoming extinct as humans spread across the planet like a virus. Some are trapped here, as we are.

"We are witches, wizards, warlocks, demons; humans have many other names for us. We inhabit their nightmares appear in their myths; they fear us, yet most claim not to 'believe' in us as if we are something they can disbelieve out of existence. We are the Anantan. The first of our race to travel here lived in what is now Spain, near Gibraltar."

Claire pauses in order to give Alexandra time to absorb what she has just learned.

"Go on, "Alexandra says.

Claire continues, "Your mother was one of the eldest of our race. She was known by many names; Nefertiti; Cleopatra; much later, Marie Laveau. When she died, people knew her as Mary Dumont. The tomb of Marie Laveau is empty. As you have always been told, your mother died 32 years ago on the day you were born."

"Cleopatra, Nefertiti?" she asks, not believing it. "But, if she was immortal, how could she have died?"

"She was not…we, are not immortal. We live centuries longer than humans; often, thousands of years longer, but, eventually physical death comes to each of us.

"Your father is an elder as well. He loved your mother from the day they first met and only wanted to be with her. She loved your father but wanted to experience everything, everyone…she was more vibrant than any being I have ever known. She had refused to settle into a life lived only with your father.

"Then, she awoke one morning and knew her time in the physical realm was nearing its end. She went to your father with a request. She wanted to have a child with him, a special child."

"In what way am I special?" Alexandra asks.

Claire says, "Let me give you a little history; something I should have done years ago. The Anantan Book of Beginnings, the Anansatya, teaches us that all of creation is woven together, like a braid. If you picture a strand of DNA, that is how they describe it. The braid forms a circle and inside the circle, that is what we perceive of as reality.

"Outside the circle, there is no time, no here, no there. It is where all spirits go when they reach full enlightenment and leave the physical plane. Some spirits choose to linger on this plane for a short time before moving on. Usually, it is because they have something important to accomplish before departing.

"For thousands of years, we traveled freely through a gateway connecting our home to other realms, including this one. There are many worlds and there were many gateways. There was only one rule. No human was allowed to go through the gate until they reached an evolutionary point equal to the beings of other realms. One of the witches broke the rule. She had been warned of the consequences but perhaps did not believe anything would happen."

Alexandra asks, "What were the consequences?"

Claire continues, "All of the gateways on this planet closed. The beautifully carved arches disappeared, replaced by pillars of stone, piles of ash. The witch and the human were lost and all travelers from other realms, including the Anantan, became prisoners here."

"So what does all of this have to do with me?" Alexandra asks.

"It was foretold in the Anansatya, the gate would be closed by an act of betrayal and could only be reopened by the key. The key is a child born to two of the elders. Our scholars have decoded the year of the birth. It is 2.7, the year in which you were born. You are a child of two elders, Lucien and Lorelei."

"So that's what Gregory meant by 'you are the key.' And Jake, is that the only reason he sought out a relationship with me?" she asks.

"I'm afraid I can't answer that," Claire says. "Although I now feel certain I was correct when I told you my suspicions about him. I believe he is a demon and once went by the name Jacques St. Germaine. I don't know how many other names he has used but I suspect thousands. He is an ancient being."

"Tell me more about demons," Alexandra says.

All eyes turn towards Claire as she answers. "Demons are the basis of the vampire myths and legends. Humans love their vampires," she says, "but no such creature really exists."

"Part of the tale comes from the ancient alchemists who knew the power of young blood. They understood how to use it to prolong a human life well beyond its normal span.

"The rest," she continues, "probably started because a demon likes to use his teeth while engaged in sex. He makes small bites all over his partner's body, barely breaking the skin."

Alexandra feels her face redden as she remembers Jake's love bites.

"Then, he runs his tongue over the wounds. The saliva is like a powerful drug. Once it enters your bloodstream, you become addicted. It is not an unpleasant feeling…at least, that is what I have been told," Claire adds hurriedly.

"Afterwards, the demon is able to control the actions, sometimes even the thoughts of his victim. That is probably the origin of the idea a vampire can raise people from the dead. His control over a victim is so strong some believe it can overcome death."

Alexandra says, "Please stop saying 'victim!' I'm not some helpless victim."

"Very well, partner, is that better? Their partners don't rise from the grave to feed on unsuspecting humans. They don't die as a result of the bites however the spell of a demon is difficult to break."

"So he is a demon and I am now under his spell. That's how he managed to control my thoughts; create my hallucinations. And he never loved me?" Alexandra asks.

"Alex," Claire says, shaking her head "a demon is rarely able to feel love. They have certain needs but…"

"Enough!"Alexandra says getting up from her chair and heading for the door.

"Alex please wait," she hears her friend Rosslyn say, but, she is already out the door. Breaking into a run, she reaches the gate and flings it open. Hearing footsteps behind her, she runs faster; so fast, she feels as if she is about to become airborne.

The only face she can see as she runs is the face of the demon she can never escape.

Finally exhausted, Alexandra slows to a walk. She is not paying attention. The man who has been following her approaches quickly and plunges the knife into her back before she has a chance to react. Collapsing to the ground, she calls his name.

CHAPTER 24

The pain comes suddenly, sending Jake to the floor.
A thousand shards of ice pierce his body. He hears her
voice calling him. Knowing she is near death is the
worst agony he has ever known.

Rising up, he bolts out of the house, forgetting he is
no longer in human form. Moving so quickly he is little
more than a rush of air as he passes people on the street,
he reaches her within minutes. Seeing her lying on the
sidewalk, so pale, he is afraid it is already too late.

He picks her up in his arms, cradling her head to his
chest. Her breath is fainter than a whisper. Not knowing
what else to do, he carries her towards the convent. He
leaps over the gate and crashes down in front of the
doorway. He sees two of the witches coming towards
him. One, he recognizes.

"Claire, please help her," he says, offering her body
up like a sacrifice.

More witches come and remove her body from his
arms. They disappear through the doorway leaving him
alone.

"What did you do to her?"

He looks up and sees Tom standing several feet
away.

"I didn't do anything," he says, "I brought her here
to save her life."

Tom demands to know what happened. "If you are
responsible, I will destroy you," he tells Jake.

"Someone stabbed her in the back. I heard her call; I
felt her pain. When I got to her, she was lying on the
street in a pool of blood. I brought her here. That is all I
can tell you," he says.

Tom orders Jake to leave the grounds. "She doesn't need you. I'll take care of her," he says.

Jake refuses. "I'll leave when she tells me to," he answers.

CHAPTER 25

The witches carry Alexandra to a room beneath the convent. Placing her face down on a table in the center of the room, they light the candles lining each wall. Claire hands each of them a robe. They join hands and form a circle around Alexandra.

Claire moves to the center beside the table. She exposes the wound in Alexandra's back. It is already inflamed.

"This was made by an evil weapon. We need to work quickly to remove the poison. Go fetch the demon," she tells Rosslyn, "and hurry."

Rosslyn rushes out and returns minutes later accompanied by Jake.

"Tell me what to do," he says.

Claire tells him the toxins need to be removed from Alexandra's wounds. He understands what that means. He goes to her and leans over her body. He places his mouth over the wound and pulls the poison out.

Falling to his knees, he spits it out, watching as it burns through the floor and into the ground.

"Quick, throw salt on this wound," he tells them. He sees they are doing as instructed before closing his eyes and falling into blackness.

Claire cleanses the wound with water taken from an ancient well and sews it closed as she recites healing incantations. She covers Alexandra with an ancient cloth believed to have great healing power. Joining the circle, she bows her head and waits.

The sun is rising when Alexandra finally opens her eyes. Not recognizing where she is, she wonders if she is

dead. Then she hears Claire's voice assuring her
everything is going to be fine.

"What happened? How did I get here?" she asks,
struggling to speak.

"Jake brought you," Claire says.

She doesn't add they are unsure if he will recover
from the part he played in saving her life. He is still on
the floor, unconscious, and Claire is unable to help him.

Smiling, Alexandra closes her eyes and is once again
asleep. The witches carry her up to her room and place
her on the bed.

Claire remains in the basement room with Jake.
Holding his head in her lap, she recites all the healing
verses she knows, but, there is no response. Finally, she
covers him with the cloth that had helped save
Alexandra and leaves him to his fate.

CHAPTER 26

Forcing his eyes open, the demon searches for some small spark of light. He is unable to tell where he is or what is happening; everything is black.

He tries to stand but finds nothing solid to hold him. He reaches out but finds nothing to grab onto. For the first time in his long existence, he experiences fear.

The void is endless, timeless and he keeps falling deeper into darkness. He closes his eyes again and conjures up visions of Alexandra. He sees her face; feels her body beneath him. "If this is the end," he thinks, "I'll go holding on to my memory of her."

He hears voices in the void, tempting him to remain. Feeling hands reaching out to grasp him, he cries out, "I won't stay. Leave me be. If I can't be with Alexandra I shall simply will myself out of existence."

Then he hears voices mocking him, saying, "The great demon Eziel feels love. What a shame. Let him go. He's useless now."

His free fall stops at last as his body hits something solid. Opening his eyes, he sees the walls of the convent cellar. He hurries up the stairs and follows the sound of friendlier voices.

Opening the door to Claire's office, he finds her there talking to Rosslyn. Relief spreads across her face. "You look like hell," she tells Jake.

"Is she…"

"She's fine. You saved her," Claire tells him.

Nodding, he closes the door and returns home to rest and regain his strength.

CHAPTER 27

Claire finds Tom in the courtyard. She tells him the news; she expects Alexandra to make a full recovery. His relief is obvious but she senses it is not entirely heartfelt. Wondering why she is detecting something beneath the surface of this seemingly ordinary man, she tells Tom it would be best if he returns to his home.

"We will certainly let you know when she is ready to have visitors. In the meantime, you should try and get some rest," she tells him.

Annoyed at being dismissed, Tom asks about Jake. "Is he still here?" he demands to know.

Claire politely tells him Jake's location is not his concern. She asks again that he leave the convent grounds.

Deciding not to make an issue of it, Tom does as she asks. Returning to the apartment, he finds Alexandra's note propped up against the empty beer glasses from the previous night.

Ripping it into tiny paper daggers, he angrily says to no one, "Farewell? Not if I can help it."

Heading for the shower, Tom hits the remote, turning on the TV. While in the shower, his fantasies return. Alexandra appears holding out her arms to him. He embraces her, kisses her naked flesh. The heat of his body turns the water to steam. His heart races as his tongue traces the curve of her breast, moves down her taut stomach.

Abruptly regaining his senses he finds he is kneeling on the floor of the shower, alone.

He dresses, grabs a beer and goes outside to sit at the patio table. It is early morning; the heat has not yet taken hold of the city. Voices carry on the still air; snippets of Cajun music come and go as cars slowly navigate the narrow streets. Revelers, returning home, pause for one last kiss before saying goodnight.

Shaking his head he thinks, "Something is happening to me, something I don't understand."

Trying to help Alexandra he has only succeeded in creating more grief for her. He feels as if his soul is being sucked away a little more each day as if he is becoming a hollow shell; a virtual human.

Confusion has become his constant state of mind. Did Jake try to kill Alexandra or did he actually save her life? Does Alexandra love Jake? Did she really have an affair with Caitlin? Even the bedrock of his love for Alexandra has been undermined.

Thinking maybe it is time for him to put all of it behind him and move on with his life, he goes inside to get another beer. Opening the drawer to retrieve the bottle opener he sees the bloody knife.

CHAPTER 28

Lucien's phone rings as he is preparing to head to The Court of Two Sisters for breakfast. Recognizing Clair's number he answers, inexplicably afraid of what he will hear.

"Lucien, it's Claire. She's all right, but, Alexandra was stabbed last night after she left us."

"I'm on my way," he says, not even taking the time to ask any questions. Somewhat surprised by the depth of his concern for his daughter, he doesn't waste time traveling by conventional means. He simply closes his eyes and imagines himself within the walls of the convent. When he opens them, he is in Clair's office.

Startled, she looks up from her desk and nods a greeting. "Lucien, don't worry. She is going to be fine. You needn't have rushed over here."

"My daughter was stabbed. I should have been protecting her. This is my fault," he says.

"Don't do this to yourself. It isn't anyone's fault. Come on, I will take you up to see her," Claire says, taking his hand and leading him up to her room.

Sleeping quietly, a look of absolute peace on her face, Alexandra is unaware of her visitors.

"She is Lorelei reborn," her father says.

"In appearance yes," Claire assures him. "Her personality, let's just say she is definitely your daughter."

Alexandra awakens. Looking up into her father's face, she feels for a moment like a child.

"Daddy? What are you doing here?" she asks.

"Where else would I be when my daughter is hurt?" he says, reaching down to brush the hair out of her eyes; eyes now filled with tears.

Perching on the edge of the bed, he asks how she is. "I'm fine. The knife wound hurts a little, but I'll be fine," she answers.

He wants to know if Alexandra has any idea who her assailant was. He seems unconvinced when she answers no. Explaining she was caught from behind and couldn't see the person's face, she can tell he is still expecting an answer.

Claire interrupts telling Lucien there is no way for her to identify the culprit.

"She's my daughter. She would not need to see the physical, only the essence. The eyes aren't necessary for that," he says. "Now, I'll ask again. Who stabbed you?"

Closing her eyes, she goes back to the previous night. She is running as fast as she can. Then exhausted, she slows to a walk. Out of breath, she can smell the fear rising off her body. A dizzy feeling is sweeping over her. She sees the face of a strange woman, then Tom, then the woman again; as if they are two sides of the same coin. She is about to turn around when she feels the blade.

It plunges deep into her back with a searing heat. Nothing has ever felt so horrible, so painful. Her spirit is wounded, her flesh infected by the evil weapon. Blinded by agony, she calls out for Jake then falls to the ground; already covered in blood.

Opening her eyes, she sees her father's furious face. Demanding to know who Tom is and where to find him he jumps up from her bed.

"Please, it wasn't his fault. I felt there was another spirit inside him; a spirit consumed with hatred for me and, for my mother," she says.

Seeing Clair's hand rush upwards to cover her mouth, she senses this description means something to the witch.

"What is it? Do you know who the woman is?" she asks.

Nodding her head, Claire answers, "Possibly; it sounds like Magdalene. But, is that possible Lucien?"

Turning to her father, Alexandra can see he recognizes the name. She asks Claire to explain.

"Magdalene was once your mother's friend but your mother had something she desperately wanted; your father's love. It drove them apart. With each year that passed, Magdalene's heart grew darker. Your father wanted to get rid of her, but, your mother refused to allow it."

Alexandra asks why. Her father answers, "Because she loved Magdalene and refused to blame her for anything."

"Then, Magdalene tried to murder your mother," Claire looks at Lucien to finish the story.

Sighing heavily, he says, "Even then your mother fought me, however, she was wounded and did not have her full strength. I don't know if I could have done what I did if that had not been the case.

"I caught Magdalene alone and in a vulnerable state. I swung my ax aiming for her neck but she was swifter than I anticipated. The blade entered her heart and killed her. Her body at least was dead, but her foul spirit escaped. I believed then that I had sent her spirit to the void, where she would remain for all eternity. Now, I think I may only have succeeded in releasing her spirit from the physical body in which it was residing."

"You tried to cut off her head?" Alexandra asks, horrified.

"It's the only way to be sure the spirit of a witch or warlock travels to the Akashic Realm. Otherwise, the spirit can escape and enter any available host, including the body of the killer," Claire explains. "Fortunately your father was strong enough to overcome Magdalene, even at the moment of her death."

Lucien says, "I realize now, her spirit must have gained possession of some living creature. She has been waiting for the opportunity to return for her revenge."

"But Tom…"

The look on her father's face is all the confirmation she needs.

"No," she says, "there must be some way to save him."

"I'm sorry Alexandra. Truly, I am," he says.

Claire and Lucien leave Alexandra to rest.

Once back in Claire's office, Lucien turns to her, saying, "How was Magdalene able to penetrate Lorelei's spell of protection and almost kill my daughter?"

Claire answers, "I wish I knew. Maybe the spell grows weaker as the time nears for Lorelei's spirit to depart. Magdalene must have had opportunities before this but the spell was still too strong to break through."

Lucien asks, "I have heard there are others looking for Alexandra; others who believe the legends of the passageways and believe she is the key. Is it true?"

"You know Lorelei believed it," she tells Lucien, "and I have no doubt there are others. I believe it is the truth. Don't you?"

"If it is…" Lucien doesn't finish his thought. He turns away from Claire and disappears.

Claire calls Rosslyn to her office to explain the relationships of Magdalene, Lorelei, and Lucien. She tells Rosslyn she and Lucien believe Magdalene is possessing the body of Alexandra's friend Tom.

"It was Tom who stabbed Alexandra," she says.

"But how is that possible?" Rosslyn asks. "Isn't she under Lorelei's protection?"

"We think the spell may be getting weaker," Claire explains. "Whatever the reason, it is imperative we keep her here."

Returning to her room to check on Alexandra several hours later Claire finds nothing but an empty bed.

CHAPTER 29

Holding the weapon in his hands, Tom is overwhelmed by the memory of wounding Alexandra. Seeing her body collapse; knowing he had inflicted the injury, had almost driven him insane.

Realizing he needs to warn Alexandra to stay away, he drops the knife and grabs his phone. He begins pressing the buttons, but the phone flies out of his hand. It hits the wall and shatters.

Frantically he searches for something with which to write. Pulling open drawers, scattering the contents onto the floor, he finally locates a pen and a scrap of paper. He begins writing his note. The paper bursts into flame.

Thinking, "If I am dead I won't be able to hurt her," he picks up the knife again. It dissolves into dust, runs through his fingers and scatters.

"Stop it!!" he screams at the enemy inside of him. "I won't let you do this!"

Racing to the door, he grabs the knob and pulls. The door won't budge. Pounding until his knuckles are bloody, he screams and curses.

He can feel the spirit inside him becoming stronger, as his will weakens. He temporarily surrenders.

Exhausted from the struggle, Magdalene guides Tom's body to the bedroom. "I will pay a visit to Gregory later, right now, I need to rest."

Observing herself in Tom's mirror, she is pleased with the reflection. Stripping, she runs her hands across the muscular chest, down the strong thighs.

"I will enjoy using the body of her beloved friend to destroy Alexandra," she thinks.

CHAPTER 30

Jake awakens again in darkness. Still shaken by his experience, he rises slowly. He is unaccustomed to the feeling of vulnerability insinuating itself into his mind; unaccustomed to feeling much of anything at all except hunger and desire.

Realizing he is famished, he assumes his human form and dresses to go out. He calls to Aaron, who responds immediately.

His relief at seeing his master is apparent. "I'm glad to see you are feeling better," he tells Jake.

"Feeling better?" Jake replies.

"Of course, my mistake," he replies. "I meant to say I'm glad your health has been restored to its former state."

"Thank you," Jake replies.

Aaron tries not to show his surprise at his master's reply. "Where would you like to dine tonight?" he asks.

Jake hesitates, unsure of whether he should go to Alexandra. She still has not contacted him; hasn't thanked him for saving her life.

"I'm not sure," he answers. It is the first time he has ever spoken these words.

"Sir, I know it's not my place but…"

"I know Aaron. I need to go to her and I will…soon," Jake says. "For now, make a reservation for me at Commander's Palace and tell them to decant a bottle of the Château Talbot St. Julian for me."

It is a long walk to the restaurant. While en route, Jake is aware of the lustful glances cast his way. His fluid appearance attracts humans of both sexes. On any other night, he would select one to enthrall, but not this night.

The maître d' shows Jake to his usual table overlooking the large oak tree. It was Alexandra who had chosen the table originally. The waiter appears and Jake orders a rare steak.

While waiting, he is approached by a gorgeous woman.

Smiling, she pulls out the chair opposite him and sits down.

"I'm Teresa," she says, holding out her hand. "And you are?"

Eyes blazing, he answers, "I am not the least bit interested in having you at my table. Please leave now."

Flustered, the woman quickly gets up, telling him he is the rudest man she has ever met. The waiter rushes over with an apology.

Jake brushes it off, saying, "Tourists, you know how they can be."

Looking towards the woman, he observes her talking animatedly to her tablemates and pointing in his direction. Something tightens in his chest. Unable to identify the cause, he chooses to ignore it and enjoy his dinner.

He has finished his meal and still, no call from Alexandra. Summoning the waiter, he asks for his check and the check for Teresa's table. On his way out, he gives her a smile and a nod. Her cheeks flush as she returns the smile.

"Now why on earth did I do that?" he wonders.

His phone begins ringing when he is almost home. The number is Alexandra's.

"Alex, I'm so glad you called," he says, relief cracking his voice.

The person on the other end is not Alexandra.

"I'm sorry Jake, this is Claire. I have some bad news. Alexandra has disappeared."

CHAPTER 31

Alexandra awakens. Her surroundings are comfortable. The moon is not visible but she can see its reflection in the water beyond her window. The sound of crashing surf echoes off the whitewashed walls. The red drapes breathe in and out. When she steps out of bed, the floor beneath her feet is cool even though the air is warm.

She is alone in the room, but she hears voices elsewhere in the house. There is the sound of music; a violin. Looking down, she sees she is dressed in a white gown. Her back is stiff. The pain of the knife wound is dull, almost imperceptible.

The dreamlike feeling of the place blurs the edges of her anxiety. Hearing footsteps approaching, she turns towards the door. A strange female enters the bedroom and smiles at Alexandra. The witch says she is glad to see Alexandra finally up and about.

"We were beginning to worry," she says in a lilting, sing-song voice, carrying hints of an African accent.

Puzzled, Alexandra asks where she is.

The witch explains they are in a house on the coast of Spain, "Cádiz to be precise," she adds.

"How did I get here?" she asks.

The witch smiles, "Your mother brought you."

"My mother is dead," Alexandra says.

Shaking her head and making a tut-tut sound with her tongue, she replies, "Your mother's spirit is very much with us. She has not yet departed for the Akashic Realm"

The witch tells her to get some more rest and she will explain everything in the morning.

"What's your name?" Alexandra asks.

"Dawn," the witch answers.

"What a lovely name," Alexandra tells her. "And this place, it has such a peaceful atmosphere…so beautiful."

"Yes. You will find it helps to heal the spirit and the body. Now, rest," she says, leaving Alexandra alone in the room with red curtains.

CHAPTER 32

Jake's frustration has reached epic proportions by the time he arrives at the convent. Assuming his natural form, he leaps over the fence and pounds on the door. Looking terrified, Rosslyn answers and leads him up to Alexandra's room on the second floor.

"What happened?" he demands to know.

Claire asks him to please return to his human form. She finds the pale turquoise skin and black eyes of the demon slightly disconcerting and not unpleasant.

Jake honors her request and asks again, "What happened?"

Claire responds saying, "We believe Alexandra was taken by her mother, Lorelei. Before she died she made a vow to protect her daughter, always. Her force is still strong; strong enough to spirit Alexandra away."

"But not strong enough to protect her from an attack," Jake replies, angrily. He asks where Lorelei might have taken Alexandra.

"That I do not know. She has connections all over the world; covens more than willing to help her," Claire replies.

"I'm sorry Jake but at least she will be safe, wherever she is. When she is able she will contact you. I feel certain of that."

She doesn't mention the spirit of Magdalene nor where they believe she is residing.

Looking dubious, Jake asks what makes her so sure.

"You are a demon and she is under your spell," Claire answers."Besides, she truly loves you."

Understanding there is nothing more he can do Jake tells Claire he will be at home if they hear anything.

"Of course, we will let you know," she says.

Turning to Rosslyn when they are once again alone, Claire says, "Let's hope he doesn't find out about Magdalene. I'm not sure he is strong enough in his current state to defeat her if it comes to a battle."

Rosslyn tells her, "I believe he suspects it was Tom who stabbed Alexandra. I'm afraid he might attempt to confront him, not knowing what he will really be up against. Maybe we should have warned him."

CHAPTER 33

Magdalene awakens refreshed. While getting dressed, she takes extra time exploring her body; reveling in its strength.

Walking to Gregory's she encounters many women who smell of desire; women yearning to feel her touch. She grants them each a smile, fanning the flames they will need to quench somewhere else.

Answering to door, Samir recognizes her immediately and rushes up the stairs to inform Gregory; his former lover has come to pay a visit.

"Is she in human form?" Gregory wants to know.

"Yes, but..."

"Send her up then," Gregory demands.

Samir does as he is told. He can hear his master's exclamation of surprise, followed by laughter.

Gregory extends his hand. "Tom, isn't it?"

Magdalene takes his hand and pulls Gregory close. "No kiss for me?" she teases.

"I think not," he answers. "Come back in a more agreeable body and we'll see."

Magdalene seats herself on the couch and asks Gregory to take a seat. "We need to talk," she tells him, "about Alexandra."

Gregory agrees. He begins by telling his story; how he had learned of Alexandra's birth from one of the Dauphine Street witches. He would not say which one.

"I believe she is the fulfillment of the prophecy. The witch also told me Lorelei died the day Alexandra was born and Lucien brought the child to live with them.

"I always believed I was the one meant to be the father of the key. I felt Lucien had stolen Alexandra from me and I began my plan to take her back as soon as she came of age.

"When I heard Eziel had begun a relationship with her, I approached him with a deal. I offered him any of my possessions in exchange for information on her. I was in for an unpleasant surprise. He refused to pass any information on to me."

He then recounts his story of sending Samir to kidnap Alexandra. "I could not have found her without his help. Lorelei's veil is thick," he tells her.

He continues, telling Magdalene how he had Alexandra in his grasp only to see her snatched away, "by her meddling father."

Magdalene advises him not to assume it was Lucien. "I believe Lorelei's spirit is still very present and it was she who took Alexandra away."

Not entirely surprised by the information, he says, "Now it is your turn. Tell me where the years have taken you and what has brought you here?"

"My spirit was lost after Lucien murdered me. I was not fully in this world nor outside of it. I was not able to escape the cycle in which I was trapped. Then Alexandra reached her age of awakening. My spirit was restored by the power within her.

"I returned to this plane and located Alexandra. I found she was in a relationship with Eziel. She did not, at that time, recognize his true nature. He was also involved in a sexual relationship with a woman in Alexandra's circle. Her name was Caitlin."

"Was? Is she no longer in the realm of the living?" Gregory asks.

"Be patient, my love. I'll explain everything." She goes on to tell Gregory how she seized the opportunity to enter Caitlin's body.

"My plan was to trick Eziel into murdering Alexandra for me. I knew Lorelei had placed a spell of protection over her, however, I hoped it would not offer protection from the demon."

Continuing, she says she did not get the chance to discover if she was correct.

"I found out, as you did, Alexandra has cast a spell of her own on Eziel. He could not bring himself to murder her as we had planned.

"I abandoned Caitlin's body and began searching for a replacement. As you can see, I found one."

"Why did the demon not recognize who was inside Caitlin's body?" Gregory asks.

Magdalene replies, "He was not looking with his eyes, only his cock."

Laughing, Gregory asks her to go on with her story. Clearing her throat, she asks if he would be kind enough to get a glass of wine for her.

"Of course," he says, rising and walking to the wine rack in the corner of the room. "What is your plea…"

The blade cleanly separates Gregory's head from his body. The ancient spirit is released; unable to ever return to corporeal form.

Magdalene is swept up into a vortex of rage. Gregory's spirit propels her around the room; slams her against the walls; crashes her body through the window. Terrified she will lose her head, she summons the physical strength in Tom's body to escape.

Grabbing hold of the door, she swings it open and rushes out of the room and down the stairs. She hears the door exploding off its hinges as she bolts into the street.

The walls of the house are expanding as Gregory's rage grows. The sound is excruciating. Covering her ears as she runs, she sees a small tornado-like shape moving away from the house in the opposite direction. She knows it is Samir.

The structure is stretched beyond its limit and the entire thing is blown apart. Bits of priceless paintings rain down on Magdalene's head; chunks of gold and silver litter the street. Then, there is silence.

Shaken, Magdalene returns to Tom's apartment. She has eliminated one obstacle from her path towards the key. Aware the news of what she has done will travel quickly she plans on leaving the country the following day.

Shedding the clothing hanging in tatters from her body, she heads for the shower. The steaming hot water electrifies her nerves. She begins fantasizing about Alexandra; the woman she despises is helpless, begging her for mercy. The scene playing out in her head leaves her aroused; unsatisfied.

Dressing quickly, she leaves the apartment. Wandering the streets, she searches for a partner; sniffing like a hound on the prowl. Finally, she encounters a luscious redhead. She smiles at Magdalene. Magdalene takes her arm and begins guiding her back to the apartment.

"Hey, hold on big guy. Don't you think maybe we should have some dinner, get to know each other?"

Magdalene stops, pulls the woman towards her and kisses her, leaving her breathless.

"All right, let's do it your way," she says, barely able to speak.

Magdalene is undressing the woman the instant the apartment door closes behind them. Carrying her into the bedroom, she tosses her on the bed and undresses, slowly, while the woman watches.

"God, you are gorgeous...those muscles," the woman whispers.

Magdalene only smiles as she climbs on top of her.

Using the woman's body to satisfy herself, she twists her around like a rag doll.

The woman begins to cry, pleading with Magdalene to take it easy, but that only excites her more. She pictures Alexandra's face as she mercilessly abuses the woman. When she is finished, the woman is unconscious.

She dresses the woman in some of Alexandra's clothes and carries her into the street, leaving the body at the curb as if she is nothing more than a bag of trash. Within hours Magdalene is on a plane headed for England.

CHAPTER 34

Jake understands what has happened to him. A demon can't escape love unscathed. His powers are weakened, but, he is still a formidable force.

Convinced Tom is the one who stabbed Alexandra, making him the one responsible for her absence, Jake is tempted to confront him immediately. Instead, he fights the urge and returns home.

Aaron is absent, undoubtedly involved in some debauchery. Jake momentarily envies his servant. He wonders what Aaron thinks about the recent changes in his master's character.

Climbing the stairs to his bedroom, he envisions Alexandra the way she looked the first time they met. She was dressed all in black; turtleneck; leggings, boots. Long jet-black hair cascaded over her shoulders. Her face was startling, like a tiny cameo mounted on a field of velvet.

He approached her cautiously afraid if he startled her she would bolt like a frightened animal. He quickly learned her diminutive form contained a woman of great depth and power. Realizing he could easily lose himself in her, he still made the choice to stay.

Now she's missing. She could be anywhere in the world.

"How am I ever going to find you?" he thinks.

He hears Aaron arriving home. Aaron sees his master on the stairs and asks about Alexandra.

"She's gone, Aaron. No one knows where."

"I'm sorry sir…Eziel."

"Just call me Jake."

CHAPTER 35

While having breakfast the next morning, Jake hears the news about Gregory. The report mentions a tall, blond man who was seen fleeing the house moments before it exploded. They are asking anyone with information to call the police.

Jake considers phoning his *friend* Detective Thibodeaux, however, he is reluctant to put himself back on the policeman's radar. He feels certain Tom is the man they are searching for. He knows no human could have done what Tom had been able to do. He wonders what spirit is using Tom's body.

Aaron brings Jake more coffee.

"Grab yourself a cup and join me," Jake tells his long-time servant.

Momentarily taken aback, Aaron recovers and joins Jake at the table.

Seated across the table from his master, Aaron feels emboldened to ask, "What's going on sir…Jake?"

"I was wondering when you would ask. There has been a change in my situation, thanks to Alexandra. She's gotten into my blood. I'm afraid I've fallen in love with her."

Aaron tries unsuccessfully to suppress a smile.

"That amuses you?" Jake asks.

"No Jake, it pleases me," Aaron replies.

"Ah, I guess it serves me right. I've infected thousands of unsuspecting humans, and non-humans, in my lifetime. Now I understand the torment I must have caused them."

"Love doesn't always mean torment, Jake. In fact, it can be quite the opposite," Aaron replies.

"Yes, well, enough of that. I want you to know you're free to go if you choose to."

Startled his master would suggest such a thing, Aaron replies, "I wouldn't think of leaving you. My life as your servant is a comfortable and happy one."

"I'm glad to hear it," Jake says. "I'd like you to pack our belongings for an extended trip. I'm not sure where we will be going so pack for all climates. I'll be closing up the house for at least several months."

"Are we going to look for her?" Aaron asks.

"No, we are going to find her," Jake replies. Aaron nods in agreement.

"Do you mind if I ask you something? It's about Caitlin."

"Of course I don't mind. What do you want to know?" Jake asks.

"Why did you go along with Caitlin's plan to murder her husband and frame Alexandra for it?" Aaron asks.

Shaking his head as if to dispel the bad memory, Jake answers, "I was afraid if I didn't go along with her, she would find someone else; someone who would gladly murder Alexandra. I felt she had become infatuated with the idea of murdering her husband and running off with his money."

"The police said she had large amounts of an antidepressant in her system when she died. Was that you?"

"Yes. I gave her an injection while she was still asleep, enough to make her very groggy but not kill her. I had enough control to force her to write the letter confessing to the murder but my power was slipping.

"I expected them to arrest her that morning and my plan was to 'visit' her in the jail cell and finish the job. I honestly don't know what caused her to collapse the way she did but she had been acting very strangely. Maybe she was ill."

"Is it possible she was possessed?" Aaron asks.

"I never thought of that but it is an interesting theory. I suspect there is an entity in possession of Tom, maybe it is the same one," Jake says.

"It could be when the entity left Caitlin she collapsed. That's when it went in search of another host and found Tom. I don't know why I didn't see this before. It would also explain why I was losing control of her."

"Where is Tom now?" Aaron asks.

"He is probably at his apartment. Maybe I should pay him a visit," Jake answers.

"Just watch yourself. Remember what happened to Gregory," Aaron advises.

Jake nods and assures Aaron he will be careful. Returning to his demon form he leaves the house.

Approaching Tom's apartment, Jake spies what appears to be a discarded pile of clothing on the curb. Recognizing one of Alexandra's blouses, he feels a moment of terror. He approaches the pile and realizes it is a strange woman, unconscious and wearing Alexandra's clothing.

Picking her up, he kicks in the door of Tom's apartment, prepared to confront him. The apartment is empty. He carries the woman into the bedroom and sets her down on the bed. Going back into the kitchen, he gets a glass of water to try and revive her.

He returns to the bedroom and finds the woman awake. She is huddled on the bed clutching her knees, trembling furiously.

"Please, please don't hurt me anymore," she says.

Jake holds out the glass, saying, "I'm not the one who hurt you. I'm just bringing you a glass of water. Please don't be afraid."

"Where is he?" the woman asks in a terrified voice.

"If you mean Tom, I don't know. He isn't here," Jake tells her.

"Please let me go. I won't tell anyone what happened," the woman pleads.

"Don't be silly. Of course, you may go, and tell anyone you want what happened. I'd like nothing more than to see that son of a bitch in jail," Jake tells her.

"So, you're not his partner? You're not going to rape me too?" she asks.

"No. As I said, you are free to go," Jake says. "I would like to ask you a few questions before you leave."

"All right," she says.

"Did he say anything at all about why he did this to you?"

"He didn't say, but, he kept calling me Alexandra and asking me to beg for my life. I did," she tells him.

"Bastard. I don't think he will be coming back. I'm going to go into the living room to see if I can find anything that indicates where he has gone. If it will make you feel better, close and lock the door behind me," Jake says.

"Thank you. I'm not afraid anymore," she says.

Jake goes into the living room to search.

The woman heads for the bathroom, leaving the bedroom door open. He can hear the shower running. For one second he considers joining her. She is very beautiful. Then he thinks of Alexandra and continues to search.

Finding nothing, he is about to leave when Tom's phone rings. The person on the other end says she is calling to confirm his reservation at Brown's Hotel in London. He tells the woman he will be there as planned.

Returning home, Jake is discussing his plans with Aaron when they hear a strange sound, like millions of birds singing with one voice. In the midst of the music, a shape appears. It is Samir.

Recognizing Gregory's servant, Jakes asks, "What can we do for you, Samir?"

"I'm sorry to intrude but, I need to ask a favor of you. I know you have great power and I would like you to use that power to help me find the one who destroyed Gregory. I was genuinely fond of Gregory and I can't let the guilty creature go unpunished."

"Do you know who did it?" Jake asks.

"Yes, it was a witch named Magdalene. She is using the body of a human man, but, I recognized her immediately," Samir tells him.

"I believe I know the man she is using as a host. His name is Tom, and, if I am correct, I know exactly where he…she is," Jake says.

"Then tell me and I will destroy him."

"I'm afraid I can't let you do that, at least not yet. I need to find out what Magdalene knows about Alexandra's whereabouts first," Jake explains.

He asks Samir to tell him about Magdalene. "I have heard the name. I know very little about the witch."

Samir explains Magdalene, like Lucien and Lorelei, is an elder. He tells Jake the three of them had been very close in their early days. "Magdalene loved Lucien but he only felt love for Lorelei. Magdalene comforted herself by entering into a relationship with Gregory."

Samir continues, "Lorelei was not willing to devote her life to one man. As the centuries passed, Magdalene watched as Lorelei broke Lucien's heart over and over again.

"She offered Lucien comfort and he didn't refuse. She mistook their sexual relationship for love. When Lorelei returned from one of her escapades and Lucien ran back to her, Magdalene became enraged and tried to kill her friend, Lorelei.

"She failed, thanks to Lucien. Then, despite Lorelei's pleas, Lucien went after Magdalene. He intended to cut off her head. In spite of her injuries, Lorelei followed and interceded. Instead of destroying her, Lucien only killed the physical body, letting loose the spirit.

"Now she is back and bent on revenge. She believes she should have been the one to have Lucien's child. She hates all of them; Lucien, Lorelei, and Alexandra," Samir concludes.

Jake says, "If she can get to Alexandra…"

"She will destroy her. I believe she has the power to do it," Samir says.

"What can we do?" Jake asks. "If we kill Tom, Magdalene will find some other body. If we cut off her head, her spirit will depart to the Akashic Realm and she will escape punishment."

Samir explains, "We need to capture her spirit at the moment of death. I can do it but I will need to be there when it happens. I can sweep her spirit up in my vortex and deliver her to the void. She will be trapped forever; unable to become one with whole, she will be alone for all time."

"Is that safe for you?" Jake asks.

Samir assures him he can dispatch Magdalene and return without risk.

"Then we will need to confront her together. Can you travel on an airplane?" Jake asks.

Samir explains he is able, but he prefers not to.

"Tell me where you will be and I will meet you there," he says.

Jake shares his information with Samir. They agree to meet at Brown's Hotel in two days. "I'll be registered under the name Jake Hollings."

"I will find you, "Samir says, and with that, he is gone.

CHAPTER 36

Alexandra dreams. She dreams of Jake; of warm days and cool nights of serenity. Opening her eyes, she sees only the room with the red curtains.

"Alexandra. It's good to see you are awake," she hears a voice, but the room is empty.

"Who are you? Why can't I see you?" Alexandra asks.

"I am Lorelei, your mother. You can't see me because I reside on a different plane. I'm here but not here."

"I can hear you though," Alexandra says.

"I could appear for you, but, it would take tremendous energy. Speaking is easier, and I have many things to tell you."

"All right, I'm listening."

Lorelei begins by telling her daughter "I love you."

"I love you too," Alexandra replies.

"I'm sorry I brought you into a world so fraught with danger. Maybe it was selfish of me but, I so wanted to have a child with Lucien. I was aware of the prophecy, but, I thought I would live long enough to teach you all you needed to know to protect yourself. I was wrong."

Alexandra asks her mother what the prophecy means; what the gateway leads to. Lorelei tells her the gateway leads to the home of the Anantans.

"It is a portal to all the realms, all but the final one," she says.

"What do I have to do?" Alexandra asks.

"I have no answer for that. The prophecy suggests you are the key. It also mentions a lock. Together the lock and the key open the gateway. Sadly, there are no clues to the identity of the lock. It could be one of us; it could be an actual lock; it could be a task you need to carry out."

Alexandra's frustration and despair are growing. "How can I even know where to begin?"

"The witches here will help you. They are an ancient and powerful coven; one of the first. They can help protect you from Magdalene as well since it appears I am no longer strong enough to give you complete protection."

Wearily, Alexandra asks if they can keep her safe from Gregory. Lorelei informs her that won't be necessary, explaining Magdalene has already eliminated him.

Suddenly fearing her enemy might have destroyed Jake as well, she asks, "Do you know if she has harmed anyone else?"

"The demon is fine. However, her spirit is in complete possession of your friend Tom. There is no way to bring him back."

"I'm not giving up on him," she replies. "You mentioned Jake. Can you tell me how to rid myself of the feelings I have for that evil creature?"

Her mother laughs, answering demons are not evil. She explains humans have always feared their kind; the witches, warlocks, demons.

"They have hunted us down through the centuries; burning us; drowning us; telling lies to their children about us. All we ever wanted was to be left alone.

"The demonkind may be selfish and lacking feeling, but they are not evil. In fact, they can be quite charming. Sadly, the race is almost extinct."

"Why is that?" Alexandra asks.

"Elementary, there are no female demons left. They found life here unbearable and one by one, they departed for the Akashic Realm. Of course, demons can mate with witches, humans, shapeshifters; but the children are not demonkind."

"Where is Jake now? Do you know?" Alexandra asks.

"I believe he is searching for you. They are all looking; Magdalene, Jake, your father."

"Why am I so hard to find?" she asks.

"Because we want you to be," her mother replies.

Alexandra asks her mother why she doesn't want Lucien to know her location.

Lorelei replies, "I love your father very much and at heart he is good but he is also selfish. He has never fully believed in the prophecy, but if his views have changed...I am afraid he would try to use you."

"Use me for what?" Alexandra asks.

Sighing, Lorelei replies, "Use you to control the gateway and all the power that would come with that."

"Was it you who spirited me away from Gregory?"

Lorelei answers, "No, and it wasn't your father. I believe you did it yourself."

Alexandra asks, "How can that be? I wouldn't know how to begin to do something like that."

"You were in danger, so you shut your eyes and pictured yourself somewhere else. It worked but then you must have become disoriented and confused. That's why you can't remember what happened."

Alexandra asks how soon she may leave the compound.

"Why are you in a rush to leave?" her mother asks. "You're safe here."

"I know, but I can't just stay here and wait for something to happen. I need to find answers. I need to find the lock and fulfill the prophecy."

Lorelei answers, "This is the best place for you to be for now. The coven will help you find the answers you need."

CHAPTER 37

Magdalene is comfortably ensconced in her suite at Brown's Hotel. She has discovered Tom is a very wealthy man. He owns the apartment building in which he and Alexandra live, along with several others. His bank accounts are large; his investments numerous.

She phones room service and orders Champagne and lobster. While waiting for the food, she studies the map of London she removed from Gregory's house. It is a specialized map which pinpoints all the covens in the British Isles. Most of the witches inhabiting them are allies of Lorelei. However, the one in Edinburgh, Scotland, is rumored to be friendly to all.

Magdalene calls the concierge and asks the woman to book her the best accommodations on the Caledonian Sleeper. The woman asks if she will be requiring a place to stay while in Edinburgh.

"Yes, of course. What do you suggest?" she asks.

"The Balmoral is the best hotel in the city, in my opinion."

"Fine. Book me a suite for Thursday through Sunday," she says.

She knows the village of Roslin is only a short distance from Edinburgh. Some Anantans believe the answer to the mystery of the lock is to be found within the walls of Rosslyn Chapel. The Chapel is the focus of many legends, but she believes in this case, the legend could be true.

Thousands of years before there was a chapel, the site was home to a coven. The coven was one of the oldest, dating back almost 10,000 years. One of the witches, Rowena, had come with the first group of travelers; those who had come from Privthi, home of the Anantan.

The stories say Rowena left the secret of the lock buried under the covenhome. After Rowena passed to the Akashic Realm, the remaining witches scattered. Eventually, the covenhome was destroyed by the elements. Magdalene believes the carvings inside the chapel reflect ancient knowledge passed down through the generations; knowledge which will allow her to control Alexandra and the gateway.

After enjoying her lunch, Magdalene heads out to visit a bookstore. Not an ordinary store, but one which allegedly holds the book she has come to London to find. But, in order to gain possession of the book, she must go through the keeper.

She remembers stories, told hundreds of years ago, of the Book of the Anantan and the one to whom it was entrusted. He was said to be a fearsome figure and one who could see into your heart, exposing the lies there.

Magdalene is sure she can handle him, persuade him to part with his treasure.

Almost invisible to passersby, the shop is nestled in a tiny alleyway off the main road with no sign to mark its presence. It is not meant to be found easily.

Magdalene walks back and forth several times before finally spotting the elusive establishment.

Opening the door, she hears a tiny bell ring announcing her presence. The man who walks through the curtain is a stranger yet she feels an immediate sense of recognition. He fills the small doorway top to bottom and side to side. His hair is mane-like in style and color. His soothing voice makes her think of standing under a waterfall; tumultuous sound in front; soothing quiet behind.

"Yes, sir? What can I do for you?" the man asks.

Momentarily forgetting she is not in female form Magdalene is taken aback. Quickly regaining her composure, she extends her hand. He does not take it. Awkwardly shoving the hand into a pocket, she explains what it is she desires.

"I have heard you have a book in your collection, an ancient book almost 10,000 years old. I would like to be allowed to see it," she says.

"I'm sorry sir, but, I don't have a 10,000-year-old book. You are misinformed," the lion-man says.

Unable to fully regain her calm demeanor, Magdalene attempts to cajole the man into allowing her access.

"You're a very handsome man," she says. "I'm sure many people have told you that. I could make it worth your time if you let me see the book."

"I am not a man who enjoys the company of other men," the proprietor says. "I think you should leave now."

"But I'm not a man. I mean, I am, but not really...I just, please, I need to see the book," she stammers.

"I don't want to hurt you, just leave, and I'll forget you were even here Magdalene," he roars.

"So you do know me. Who are you?" Magdalene asks.

Appearing to grow larger and more frightening, the man again tells her to leave."I see the evil within you. Stop your quest now and depart this realm!"

"Not until I see Alexandra destroyed!" she shouts as she leaves the shop and returns to the hotel.

CHAPTER 38

Jake and Aaron are in a taxi on the way to Brown's Hotel when Jake's phone rings. It is Alexandra's number but he knows the phone is in Claire's possession.

"Hello, Claire. Is anything wrong?" he asks.

"No, everything is status quo. I thought you might have some news," she replies, sounding exhausted.

"Aaron and I are in London. We're headed for Brown's. We know Tom is there."

Sounding worried, Claire says, "Jake, there's something you don't know about Tom..."

"If you mean that he is possessed by the spirit of Magdalene, I know," Jake tells her.

"Oh, then I guess you already know what you are dealing with," Clair says, sounding relieved.

Jake explains how Samir had paid a visit to the house on Royal after Magdalene dispatched Gregory.

"He explained why Magdalene is bent on destroying Alexandra."

"I know I can't talk you out of confronting him, just please be careful," Claire says.

Laughing, Jake replies, "It's nice to know you're concerned for me. We'll be careful and I will call when I have something to report."

"Do you think Magdalene is still here?" Aaron asks, after Jake completes his call.

Jake tells his Aaron he expects to find Magdalene at the hotel.

"However, even if she has already checked out, someone at the hotel may know where she is headed," he says.

"One way or another, we will locate her."

Checking in, Jake is impressed by Magdalene's choice. The quiet, old-world elegance of the hotel is reminiscent of New Orleans, minus the sweltering heat.

Smiling at the man behind the desk, he asks if his colleague Tom Bouchard has checked in yet.

"We have a business meeting first thing tomorrow," he explains.

The man smiles back, wishing he could have a meeting of another type with Jake. Checking his computer screen, he tells Jake, "Yes. Your colleague checked in two days ago."

"Excellent. Thank you," Jake says.

"It's my pleasure. Please let me know if there is anything at all I can do to make your stay more enjoyable," the clerk replies, touching Jake's hand as he gives him the keycard.

Accompanied by a bellman, Jake and Aaron take the elevator up to their rooms on the third floor.

"Come to my room once you are unpacked," Jake tells his assistant.

Once settled in his room, Jake picks up the phone and calls the front desk. He asks to be connected to Tom's room. There is no answer. He is debating whether to flirt with the clerk in order to get the room number when Aaron arrives.

"I did a bit of sniffing around. Magdalene is on the fifth floor. She is not in the room right now, if you would like to pay a visit," he tells Jake.

"Yes, let's do that," he says. He throws open the door and discovers Samir, hand up, about to knock.

"Ah, the last musketeer has arrived. We were just about to go and check out Magdalene's suite," Jake says.

"All right, lead the way," Samir answers.

The three take the elevator to the fifth floor. Concentrating intently on masking themselves from view, they make their way to Magdalene's suite unseen. Samir enters and unlocks the door for the other two.

Once inside they begin combing the room for any clues that might help them decipher why the witch has come to London. Frustrated after 20 minutes of searching, they are about to give up when Jake spots a corner of paper sticking out from under the desk pad.

Pulling it out, he sees it is a map, a very old map.

"Look at this," he says to his companions. "It has the locations of all the covens in this area. Magdalene must by contacting all of them, attempting to find Alexandra."

"It's a start, but, it still doesn't tell us why she came here. There are covens all around the world," Samir points out. "Why come to London?"

"You're right," Jake says. "Let's wrap this up for now and head out for some dinner. I can think better on a full stomach."

Walking by the reception desk, Jake sees the flirtatious clerk waving him over.

"Mr. Hollings, I'm so glad I caught you. I'm afraid I may have given you some bad information regarding your friend. He did check in yesterday, but, he is leaving tonight for Edinburgh. He must have forgotten about your business meeting."

"That idiot!" Jake says. "How does he expect me to handle this alone? Now I'll have to reschedule. Do you know when he is due back?" Jake asks.

"He has the room here until next Wednesday but, I'm not sure when he is returning."

"Thanks. You're a sweetheart for letting me know," Jake says, flashing the clerk his best grin.

The three companions head across the street to an Indian restaurant. The aromas wafting out the front door are promising. Once seated, they discuss whether or not it is worthwhile making the trip to Scotland.

"We know she is coming back here. Why not visit some of the covens while she's gone; see if we can find out anything," Aaron says.

"I think you're right. It will give us time to prepare for the confrontation," Samir agrees and Jake approves of the plan.

During their meal, Jake asks Samir how he had come to be associated with Gregory.

"Thousands of years ago, I lived in a land known as Tarab-ay. I believe it is now referred to as Iran. I fell in love with a witch named Terpsichore. The music we created together filled the sky with color; filled hearts with joy. She gave substance to my song.

"I knew from the beginning she was promised to a powerful warlock, however, knowing could not overcome desire. We ran off together, foolishly hoping the strength of our love would protect us."

Samir pauses as the horror of the event returns to him. He continues, "It did not. Her father found us and beheaded his daughter as I watched, helpless to stop him. He had brought the one weapon over which a wind wraith has no power. He cast a spell creating a prison of ice and locked me inside.

"I would have remained eternally frozen if Gregory hadn't come upon us and observed what was happening. He took pity on me and freed me from my icy cell. He sent the warlock to the Akashic Realm to rejoin his daughter. From that day until the end of days, I will remain indebted to him. I cannot rest until his murderer is punished."

Jake says, "I am sorry for your loss. No matter how much time has passed, the wound must feel fresh to you."

Nodding, Samir answers, "I still listen for her song every day."

CHAPTER 39

Alexandra awakens. Feeling whole and healthy, she has healed quickly. Climbing out of bed she goes to the window. Pulling back the red curtains, she sees the sea is calm; the day slightly overcast.

Hearing the door open behind her, she turns to find Dawn entering the room. Smiling, she asks about breakfast.

"I feel as if I haven't eaten in months," Alexandra tells her.

Dawn tells her to get dressed, come downstairs for breakfast and she can meet the other residents.

"We are preparing to have our morning meal. It will be a good opportunity for everyone to welcome you," she says.

The room where the witches are gathered for breakfast is open on three sides, providing unobstructed views of the water. The air is cool and smells of salt blended with the citrusy aromas of orange and lemon. Under different circumstances, Alexandra muses, she could happily wake up here every morning.

Taking a seat next to Dawn, Alexandra listens as each witch is introduced. She knows she will never remember the names, but, smiles and nods to each one. There are 13 in all, including Dawn. Oleander, the one seated to Alexandra's left asks how she is feeling.

"Much better than I anticipated," she answers. "This place is magical; the air; the ocean; all of you. It would have taken months for me to recover if I had stayed in New Orleans."

The witch nods in agreement. "This is a special place," she agrees.

"My mother came to me when I first arrived here. We spoke for a short time and she told me you are an ancient coven. She said you would be able to help me find some answers," Alexandra says.

None of the witches appear to be surprised at the news of Lorelei's visit.

Oleander replies, "Of course we will help you. All the Anantan want to solve the riddle of the prophecy. Sadly, some only want to use it to further their own ambitions; increase their wealth.

"We are interested in knowledge for the sake of knowledge. If the gateway allows us to travel freely once again, our store of information will be greatly increased. The things we could learn! It is almost unimaginable."

"Where do you suggest I begin?" Alexandra asks.

Dawn answers, "We have heard there is a store in London which houses a book; a book which tells the story of the Anantan from the time of our arrival to the present. Allegedly, it gives a clue where to look for the lock. The owner is a warlock and very difficult to deal with but if he likes you he will allow you a glimpse of the book. If you like, we can travel there together as soon as you feel up to it."

Alexandra tells her, "I feel up to it now. How soon can we leave?"

Dawn tells her there are a few matters she must take care of first. "We can leave in the morning," she says. "It is a short flight."

"Flight?" Alexandra asks with apprehension. "Can't we just will ourselves there?"

Dawn answers, smiling, "Yes but, that sort of travel is very taxing. We prefer to let the airplanes do the work. Is that a problem?"

"No…no, of course not," Alexandra replies. "It's just not my favorite way to travel."

Alexandra decides she will spend the day exploring the town to take her mind off the upcoming flight. Dawn suggests a visit to the Cádiz Cathedral.

"You can easily spend a day there exploring the cathedral and the surrounding area. You'll enjoy it. It will do you good to play tourist and relax for a few hours."

Alexandra agrees a complete escape from reality is exactly what she needs.

CHAPTER 40

Alexandra is on the roof of the cathedral admiring the view of the sea. Shivering suddenly as if cold hands have grabbed her by the shoulders, she spins around.

The man towers over her. His expression is neither friendly nor hostile but Alexandra is aware of her vulnerable position.

He puts her fears to rest when he begins speaking. His voice is not what she expected. Instead of loud and overpowering, it cradles her; soothes her worries.

"Don't be afraid. I didn't come here to hurt you," he says. "I know what you are and I have something that could help you but I need to be sure you are the one."

"What can I do to assure you?" Alexandra asks.

"Come with me," he says, holding out his hand.

Hesitantly, Alexandra takes his hand. She feels the air inside her rushing out. She is no longer standing on the roof of the Cathedral. Instead, she is suspended in space. Around her stars and planets are rushing past, becoming mere suggestions of shapes.

She is losing all sense of where she begins and ends. A profound sense of connection is the only feeling. There is no fear, no holding on to what was left behind.

She is almost beyond the point of no return when abruptly she finds herself back on the roof. The man is gone. In his place is a book with a worn leather cover. There are no markings on the outside. It is thick yet feels light as air when Alexandra lifts it.

Thumbing through the pages, she thinks she will never be able to decipher it. It is written in an ancient language unfamiliar to her. Then as she watches, the letters resolve themselves into recognizable words.

Dropping to the floor she begins to read.

*"It is the year zero. It is the beginning. We are the
Anantan, explorers, wanderers. We are 30 in number.
We have left behind our realm and all that we know to
explore this new reality. We are the first.*

*"The two-legged animals here are primitive and
avoid any contact with us. The air is clean and smells of
earth and salt. We are close to a huge body of water.*

*"The temperature is suitable for us. We are able to
travel about with little protection from the elements.*

*"We have agreed 10 of our party will remain here;
five will go East; five West; five South and five North.
We hope to reunite some day. This book we leave with
Simha. May he guard it well."*

Alexandra thumbs through the next several pages
which are filled with drawings of flora and fauna from
the area. She continues reading.

*"I am Simha. The book has been given to me. I have
chosen to join Rowena and the group of travelers
headed north.*

*"We are anxious to explore this place and have
made the decision to walk until we find a suitable place
to settle.*

*"The four-legged creatures we encounter
everywhere are friendly and allow us to approach them.
They will accept food from the females among us. Some
have even begun to follow in our tracks.*

*"Rowena has spotted a large one, black and white,
who appears to be the leader. She will attempt to climb
on the creature's back tomorrow. If she succeeds, we*

may all try to mount and ride the creatures, making our long journey less tiring.

"Rowena was successful. The creature, which she has named Shadrach, willingly carried her weight. He allowed himself to be guided by her body movements. The two appeared to become one as they raced across the open fields. Rowena returned and praised the creature's strength and intelligence.

'They will carry us on our journey,' she tells us. 'Each of you must find the proper mount, one you feel a bond with.'

"We four went up into the hills and spent many days and nights following the group. One by one, my three companions found suitable mounts. I was the last.

"I came upon my creature standing beneath a waterfall. He is larger than the others and black as the night sky. I held out my hand and he came to me. He chose me. I asked for his name. He lifted his head upwards. I followed his gaze and I saw the sphere we call Janus. So he was named.

"Rejoining the group, I ask Rowena if she can see where we will eventually end our journey. She is a time seer; able to see past, present, and future as one.

"Nodding she answers, 'Yes. One day, the gateway will reopen where we make our home.'

"I ask what she means. 'The gateway is open and I see no reason for it to close,' I say.

"She tells me many Anantan will follow in our footsteps, but one will betray us all and cause the destruction of the gateway. It will remain out of our sight for many thousands of years until one day a key will be given, a key that will restore the gateway.

"That is all she will tell me, no matter how much I beg her for more of the story. Perhaps I will see the story unfold before my own eyes."

The book goes on to tell of the travels of the Anantan. Alexandra comes to a section that describes a great statue of Simha built in a desert kingdom. There is a drawing of what is very obviously the Sphinx as it was in the beginning before much of it was buried in the shifting sands. She wonders how many drawings and carvings of wondrous beasts of the ancient world were really inspired by the Anantan. She continues reading.

"Today we crossed paths with travelers from another realm. They told us some from their party had traveled across the water and settled on an island they call Atal-Antas. Claiming they have created a glorious city much like the ones we left behind, we are doubtful.
They say, 'Go and see for yourselves,' but we tell them we have our own cities to build."

Her reading is interrupted by a young couple arriving on the roof to enjoy the view. They apologize but she assures them she was about to leave and, gathering her belongings, she heads down the steps. It is already late in the afternoon and Alexandra finds herself thinking of the coven and looking forward to her return. It has already begun to feel like home.

Arriving at the whitewashed building which houses the coven, Alexandra seeks out Dawn to ask what she makes of the mysterious book and the strange man who gave it to her. She finds her in the main room studying a map.

"What's this?" she asks Dawn.

"It is an ancient map of the area that is now the British Isles," Dawn tells her.

"But that doesn't look like an island. It is attached to the mainland," Alexandra says.

"I guess they didn't teach you ancient geography in that college you attended," Dawn says, laughing. "The British Isles used to be a peninsula. This is the approximate area of one of the first covens. It's near Rosslyn Cathedral."

The mention of Rosslyn reminds Alexandra of her old friend. It feels like she has lived a lifetime since the last time they were together.

Dawn notices the book Alexandra is clutching and asks what it is.

"This is the reason I was looking for you," she says. "A very odd man…warlock…honestly, I don't know what he was, gave it to me. It is a history of the Anantan on this planet, at least that's what he claimed."

Grabbing the book, Dawn quickly scans the pages.

"This is it," she says, excitedly. "This is the book I was telling you about. Where did this man come from? How did he find you?"

Holding her hands up to stop the stream of questions, Alexandra says, "I don't know and I don't know. I was on the roof of the cathedral and he suddenly appeared. He took my hand and I felt like I was lost in space like I was dissolving into infinity. He pulled me back from the edge, then handed me the book and disappeared."

Dawn flips to the end of the book. With a shocked expression, she hands the book back to Alexandra.

Pointing to the last page she says, "Look at what it says."

Taking it, Alexandra looks at the page. It says, "You are the key. The book of the Anantan is yours. You are the chosen." It is dated Year 0.

Shocked, Alexandra says, "So it is true. I guess I didn't really believe it before."

"We need to study this. The answer is in here."

Alexandra asks, "Are we still going to England, now that we have the book?"

"I don't know. Let's study it first then decide," Dawn says.

They sit down together in the room overlooking the sea. Alexandra takes the tome and begins reading aloud. Before long, they are joined by the other members of the coven. It is dark by the time she finishes. Candles have been lit, glasses of wine poured.

"So it seems the answers we are searching for will be found in Scotland," Alexandra says as she closes the book.

CHAPTER 41

Jake, Aaron, and Samir have visited almost every coven within a 100-mile radius of London. None of the witches have heard from Magdalene; none have heard from Alexandra. The last place they visit is a small coven located in Epsom.

There they encounter a witch who claims to have arrived with the first group of travelers from Privthi. Her name is Esmeralda.

Informing the trio she has not heard anything from Alexandra, she adds, "We did have a visit from Magdalene, hiding in the body of a human man. She also asked about Alexandra, but we gave her no information. We had none to give and wouldn't have shared it with her in any case. She is an evil spirit."

Excitedly Jake asks if Esmeralda knows why Magdalene chose to come to England.

"Yes, I know. She is searching for a book," Esmeralda says.

Confused, Jake asks what book could possibly be so important.

"Allow me to explain. When we first arrived here, one of my group, Simha, began keeping a journal. It is the history of the Anantan here on Gaia, or Earth as the humans call it. Simha pledged to be not only the keeper but the chronicler. He gathered news of the Anantan as he traveled and added it to the history.

"He is in London and, to the best of my knowledge he is still in possession of the book, perhaps still adding to it. It is not an easy task to persuade him to part with information. If he likes you, he will tell you anything. If he doesn't…you will be lucky to escape with your life.

"We heard Magdalene visited him but came away empty-handed. Here is the address. If you go, go with care."

Taking the paper from Esmeralda's hand, Jake thanks her profusely.

Esmeralda shakes her head, "No need to thank me. I know the story of Magdalene and Lorelei; and Lorelei's child. If she is the key to our gateway home, I will do anything I can to help you find her."

Jake asks, "What do you mean the key to a gateway home?"

Surprised, Esmeralda asks Jake if he is unfamiliar with the history of how the Anantan had come to Gaia, and Alexandra's part in helping them all to return home.

"I've heard the history of the gateways. I've also heard the legend of the key, but I don't see what that has to do with Alexandra."

Shaking her head, she replies, "Do you think we are all concerned with Alexandra's safety simply because she is the charming child of Lucien and Lorelei?"

"What other reason could there be?" Jake asks, becoming concerned.

"You still don't understand? Alexandra is the key; at least that is what most of us believe," Esmeralda tells him.

Shaken by the news, Jake turns to Samir. "Did you know about this?" he demands.

Nodding, Samir answers, "Yes. I assumed you did as well, my friend."

Angrily, Jake responds, "Well, I did not. So it's not just Magdalene we have to worry about."

Esmeralda hesitates before telling Jake there are many who search for Alexandra.

"Her father is also looking for her…and there could be others as well. The one who controls the passages will possess great power.

"That is why it is imperative you visit Simha as soon as possible," Esmeralda says.

The three express their gratitude again and decide to spend the night in Epsom before heading back to confront the formidable Simha.

"At least these past two days have not been a total loss," Jake says. "If we can get Simha to talk to us, he may be able to help us find Alexandra."

Samir looks doubtful. "I know this creature," he says. "He is unlike the rest of you. He will not be swayed by charm, or wit or even your good intentions. He can see clear through to the heart of the matter and if he doesn't like what he sees, he may kill you, just as Esmeralda said."

"I can go alone," Jake says. "I don't see any reason for all of us to take the risk."

Samir assures Jake, Simha's power is no threat to him.

"I will not let you go without me, "Aaron adds. "It's three or none."

"So it's settled. We will go together tomorrow," Jake says.

Once his companions have gone to their rooms, Jake prepares to leave for London alone. He writes a note for Aaron saying, "I will meet you tomorrow at Brown's Hotel. Tell Samir I appreciate his help, but, this one I need to do alone. I will see you soon my friend."

CHAPTER 42

Still seething from her treatment at the hands of
Simha, Magdalene spends most of her time in Scotland
aimlessly roaming the streets of Edinburgh. She hasn't
visited the nearby covens or Rosslyn Chapel.

She is on another fruitless walk when her phone
rings. It is Azurine, one of the witches from the Epsom
coven. Magdalene had met Azurine on her visit to
Epsom. None of the witches there had heard anything of
Alexandra but they invited Magdalene to stay for the
night.

Esmeralda recognized Magdalene behind the visage
of Tom. She put forth the invitation to stay hoping to
learn something of value from the witch.

One of the younger members of the coven
volunteered to spend time with her. She claimed it
would be in an effort to make Magdalene relax and let
her guard down. Esmeralda feared the young witch was
attracted to the handsome man.

Azurine offered to take Magdalene on a tour of the
surrounding area. Despite knowing Tom was possessed
by the female spirit, Azurine could not ignore the
attraction she felt. The two strolled the streets together
arm in arm. Azurine led her away from the town and up
into the hills. They found a secluded spot and made love
in the open air, gazing at the stars.

Magdalene enjoyed the body of the young witch, her
soft skin, and gentle touch. She was briefly able to
forget everything and become the caring soul she had
once been.

Preparing to leave the next morning, she pulled
Azurine aside.

"If you hear anything of Alexandra or if anyone comes looking for her, you are to call me. Here is my number," Magdalene told her.

"I promise. Will you be returning?" Azurine asked.

"I don't know. Would you like me to?" Magdalene responded.

"You know I would," Azurine said, taking Magdalene's hand and placing it on her breast.

Pulling away, Magdalene replied, "We'll see."

Now, Azurine is calling, hopefully with good news.

"Hello, Azurine. Do you have information for me?" Magdalene asks.

"Yes. Three travelers visited here today. They were asking about Alexandra," Azurine tells her, feeling torn between guilt and lust.

"Very good. Do you know their names?" she asks.

"Jake, Samir, and Aaron," the witch answers.

"Perfect! Don't let them leave," she commands.

"Don't worry. They have already said they are spending the night in town."

"I will see you later. Don't say a word to anyone," Magdalene tells her.

"Will you make it worth my while?" Azurine teases.

Magdalene promises she will.

Feeling a rush of anticipation, Magdalene wills herself back to Epsom not having time to travel by conventional means.

Locating the inn where the three are staying, Magdalene is about to enter when she sees Jake leaving. He is in his demon form. He is alone.

Sensing his power is still too strong for her, she decides to go after his weaker companion.

Magdalene cloaks herself and enters the inn.

Hunting for the scent of Jake's assistant, she locates him and enters his room undetected.

Staring down at his handsome face, she momentarily regrets what she is about to do. She is aware the wind wraith is close by. She can't afford to waste any time.

Aaron's eyes fly open as she swings the knife, removing his head.

There is no maelstrom as there was with Gregory. Aaron's passage to the Akashic Realm is peaceful.

Grabbing his phone on her way out, Magdalene dials Azurine's number.

"I'm on my way," she says. "Meet me in front of the covenhome."

Azurine is waiting outside as Magdalene instructed.

Grabbing the young witch around the waist, Magdalene pulls her close, kisses her deeply.

Azurine responds, urging Magdalene to follow her upstairs to the bedroom. Magdalene refuses, asking instead how far it is to the stone circle known as the Coldrum Long Barrow.

Confused, Azurine answers, "About 80 kilometers. Why?"

Annoyed at being questioned, Magdalene replies, "That's where I want to make love to you, that is why. Are you able to transport yourself or do we need to drive there in the car?"

Upset by the gruff reply, Azurine answers she is able to get to the spot under her own power.

"Then let's go," Magdalene says, and disappears.

Unsure now about what she has done, Azurine waits a few minutes before following. She finds Magdalene angrily pacing the ground.

"What kept you?" she demands to know.

Instead of answering, Azurine sheds her clothes and approaches Magdalene.

Somewhat mollified, Magdalene tells the young witch to dance for her. Seating herself on the ground, Magdalene watches appreciatively as the beautiful young witch twirls and undulates before her. Cupping her breasts she sidles forward then spins away.

Magdalene undresses and approaches Azurine from behind. Pulling the witch's body close she fondles her, feeling the heat rising off her body.

They fall together. As Magdalene enters Azurine the ground begins to shake; lightning streaks across the black sky. Forgetting herself, Magdalene allows Azurine to see the witch inside Tom's body.

Terrified by the twisted, angry visage, Azurine tries to escape. Regaining control, Magdalene retreats and Tom's face returns.

Magdalene smothers the young witch with kisses and Azurine responds with heightened desire. Thunder rolls across the hills as Magdalene collapses, finally satiated.

"I know where to find her now," Magdalene says.

Confused, Azurine asks what she means.

"This place, our bodies together; we broke through the veil surrounding Alexandra. I briefly saw her thoughts. I know where she is," Magdalene tells her.

Angry at being used, Azurine gathers her clothes and prepares to leave.

"That's all this was? You just wanted me to help you find this other witch?" she spits out. "You'll regret this."

Furious, Magdalene exposes her true face again and turns on the young witch.

"Don't you dare threaten me. You have no idea with whom you are dealing. Go now, before I forget the pleasure you've given me."

Azurine retreats back to the covenhome, distraught and in tears. Magdalene lingers on the barrow imagining the things she will do to Alexandra before murdering her.

"And it won't be a beheading, that's too good for her. A dagger to the heart is more like it. Then she will spend eternity in darkness, as she deserves."

CHAPTER 43

The journey to London is an easy walk for the
demon. While he travels, he thinks of Alexandra. He
wonders if she dreams of him as constantly as he dreams
of her. The pain of loneliness is a new experience for
him, one he is not enjoying.

The sun is rising when Jake arrives in the city. He
has memorized the address and the route. He has no
trouble locating the small building almost hidden in the
alleyway. The lights of the shop are on in spite of the
early hour.

Approaching the door, he sees it is already opening.
The creature in the doorway is extraordinary. Jake has a
brief moment of fear, but it is quickly put to rest when
Simha speaks.

"Please come in, Eziel. I have been expecting you,"
he says.

Entering the small shop, Jake is overwhelmed by a
feeling of longing. The place is filled with Anantan
artifacts. The aroma of Pratika blossoms permeates the
air.

"Is this what it's like to feel homesick for a place
you have never seen?" Jake asks the giant.

"So you have feelings now. It is because of
Alexandra, yes?" Simha asks.

Jake nods, "It is. It's the reason I have come to you. I
need help. I need to find her before Magdalene does."

Simha nods his head. "I know. I have already given
the book to Alexandra. I expect she is on her way to
Scotland if she is not there already."

Puzzled, Jake asks why Scotland.

"The answer you seek is there. That's all I can tell you. Now that I have completed my task, at last, it's time for me to move on to the final realm. Good luck," he says to Jake, and then he is gone.

All traces of Privthi disappear with Simha. Jake looks around and sees only an ordinary bookshop. Heading back to the hotel, he wonders if Magdalene has found any answers on her trip to Scotland. It seems to be the nexus of the mystery.

While walking to the hotel, Jake's phone begins to ring. He sees it is Aaron.

"Hey Aaron I was just about to call," he says.

"Guess again Eziel," he hears the voice on the other end say.

"Who is this? Where is Aaron?" Jake asks angrily.

"My, we sound upset. I thought demons didn't have feelings but it sounds as if you are concerned about your little slave," the voice taunts him.

"Magdalene, is that you?" Jake shouts into the phone.

"Good guess demon, but, it wasn't very hard to figure out was it?" the voice of Tom asks.

"Listen to me, you piece of shit, if you do anything..." He doesn't get the chance to finish. Magdalene has hung up on him.

He looks up and discovers he is in front of the hotel.

His flirtatious friend is behind the desk.

"Mr. Hollings it's so good to see you again," he gushes.

Jake gives him a big grin. "Good to see you too," he says. "Has my wayward friend returned yet?"

"No, sir. He is due back tomorrow though," the clerk tells him.

Heading up to his room, Jake wonders where Samir is. He doesn't think Samir would have tried to take on Magdalene alone. Maybe Magdalene got to him first and caught him off guard. Shaking his head to dispel the negative thoughts, Jake opens the door to his room and immediately finds the answer to his question.

"Samir, it's good to see you are all right. We need to return to Epsom right away. Magdalene has Aaron," Jake says.

"I know Jake. I'm sorry," Samir says.

"Don't be sorry. We can handle her and get Aaron back but we need to hurry," Jake says excitedly.

"Jake, I'm sorry. It's too late," Samir says.

"What are you talking about? What do you mean 'too late'?"

"He's gone, Jake. Magdalene murdered him in his sleep. He wasn't powerful enough to see her coming or to stop her. He has gone to join the one in the Akashic Realm," Samir says, watching as his companion sinks to his knees in grief.

"It's my fault. All of this is my fault." The words are torn out of Jake's throat as molten rivers of tears flow down his cheeks.

"It is not your fault. Even if you had been there, you couldn't have stopped it and she may have gotten to you too. I know you will miss him but we need to go on with our plan. We need to destroy this monster."

Jake wipes the burning tears away. "You're right. She is a monster and we will stop her before she destroys anyone else. But, how did she know where to find us?"

"I suspect one of the witches in Epsom betrayed us," Samir says.

"We'll have to revisit that coven when all of this is over," Jake says.

"Did you find Simha?" Samir asks.

Jake is still trying to pull himself together to answer Samir when his phone begins to ring.

CHAPTER 44

In the days following Alexandra's disappearance from New Orleans, Lucien had desperately searched for her. His mind reached out to witches and warlocks all across the globe but to no avail. She was, and is, invisible to him.

He is convinced it is his beloved Lorelei keeping her hidden. He is aware she doesn't trust him, and perhaps she is right not to. He loves his daughter and would never do anything to hurt her. He also loves his power and if the legends are true, Alexandra can help him increase that power immeasurably.

His frantic searching has alerted his enemies, human, warlock, and others, to his Achilles Heel. They know about Alexandra and even those who do not believe the legends understand she is a weapon to be used against Lucien.

He has amassed many enemies during his long life. From some he has stolen great sums of money; from others, loved ones. He has sent many to the Akashic Realm.

He does not regret his past, nor is he afraid of his future. Instead, he fears for the safety of his daughter.

Trying to contact Magdalene has proven fruitless. Shutting him out of her mind, she has remained elusive.

Increasingly frustrated, he finally contacts Claire and asks if she has heard any news.

"Have you heard anything regarding Alexandra's whereabouts?" he asks her.

Sighing, she responds, "No. I was hoping you were calling to give me some news. I am sure you heard about Gregory?"

It is more of a statement than a question.

Lucien responds that he has heard of Gregory's demise. "Was it Magdalene?" he wants to know.

"I believe it was. I heard a rumor that she has left the country," Claire says.

Lucien asks if she has spoken to Eziel. "Not recently," she says.

"Give me his number," Lucien commands. "I will call and find out if he knows anything."

Claire gives him the number and is about to ask if he will be leaving the country as well when she realizes he has already ended the call.

Dialing Jake's number, Lucien waits impatiently for him to answer. The call goes to voicemail instead.

"Eziel, this is Alexandra's father. Please let me know where you are. I would like to meet with you so we can devise a plan to find my daughter," he says.

Across the Atlantic, Jake listens to Lucien's message. Samir can see he is not happy with what he is hearing.

"Is everything all right?" Samir asks.

"Lucien would like to meet with me so we can come up with a plan to find Alexandra. I don't trust him," Jake tells Samir.

"So you are not going to call him back?" Samir asks.

"It's not in my plans to do that," he says.

CHAPTER 45

Alexandra awakens. She is aware of her mother's presence. The aroma of sandalwood is overwhelming. She senses sadness in her mother's spirit. Confused, she sits up in bed and lights the candle on her bedside table. The curtains are sighing softly. She waits for her mother to speak.

"Alexandra, my darling daughter, I have come to say goodbye," Lorelei says.

"Goodbye? I don't understand. There is still so much I want to know. I have so many questions," Alexandra cries.

Lorelei replies, "I know my sweet, but my time is growing short. If I don't depart this realm soon I will be trapped here forever."

Anguished, Alexandra asks, "Can't you just possess someone like Magdalene does? Wouldn't that give you more time?"

"Possession is an evil act. It deprives a spirit of its rightful host. It damages the spirit of the possessor.

"Magdalene was once a kind and loving witch. Her jealousy ate away at her; her possession of Caitlin, then Tom, has destroyed any goodness she had left. I would not walk that same path.

"I feel my hatred for her growing. If I were to enter another body now, I fear it would be the end for me.

"Can you understand?" she asks her daughter.

Sighing, Alexandra tells her, "Of course. I was being selfish. After spending so many years without you, I just wanted a little more time. I'm scared, mother, afraid and unsure what to do."

Lorelei's spirit approaches Alexandra. Reaching out to her daughter, Alexandra feels a warm breeze gently stroking her.

"You have many friends. Your demon will find you soon, and the witches here are all ready to help you any way they can. The book has given you many answers. Just follow your instincts. I believe in you," Lorelei tells her daughter.

Alexandra tearfully asks, "Can't I see you just once before you leave?"

Lorelei summons all of her remaining strength and appears before her daughter.

"You are so beautiful," Alexandra says, reaching out to embrace her mother. "Thank you for this."

As they hold one another, Lorelei's spirit fades.

Alexandra knows her mother has departed for the Akashic Realm.

"I love you mother. Someday I will follow you and we will have eternity to be together," Alexandra says.

Unable to sleep, Alexandra wanders down to the common room. Gazing out over the sea, she thinks about what her mother had said. "Your demon will find you soon."

She thinks, "Now that my mother is gone, maybe the veil of secrecy will dissipate. I wonder if that means my father and Magdalene will be able to find me too. I wish she had explained it all to me."

Hearing someone approaching from behind, she turns to find Dawn.

"She came to say goodbye to me too," she tells Alexandra.

"There was so much I wanted to learn from her," Alexandra says. "Why did she never contact me before? We could have had more time."

"Each manifestation weakened her ability to stay in this realm. She was always watching over you, but, she waited until you had urgent need of her before making contact. You need to understand she put herself at risk to help you," Dawn tells her.

Alexandra asks how she was at risk.

"If Magdalene had found her while she was in a vulnerable state, she could have prevented her from ever joining the one. Now she is safe for all time until the end of time."

Alexandra asks Dawn when she thinks they should make their journey to Scotland.

"You have been through so much and you will need all your strength if we are to be successful. We should wait a few more days at least."

Alexandra nods in agreement. "This place is good for my spirit," she says. "I will gladly stay a few more days."

CHAPTER 46

Packing a single bag, Jake leaves Brown's Hotel. He stops at the desk on his way out, telling the clerk he will be back in a few days, alone. He tells the clerk his assistant Aaron has already returned to New Orleans. The words cause a lump to form in his throat. The new emotions Jake is experiencing are not pleasant.

"When do I get to feel something enjoyable?" he asks Samir as they hail a cab to take them to the airport.

"Ah my friend, now you sound almost human," Samir replies.

"No need to be rude," Jake answers.

The flight to Edinburgh is short but it gives Jake enough time to decide their first move.

"Are you sure your presence aboard the plane is safe?" Jake asks Samir.

"Fairly sure, yes," Samir answers.

"I guess that will have to do," Jake says. "According to the map we found in Magdalene's room, the coven in Scotland is ancient. I think we should start with a visit there. Simha didn't say what it is we are looking for or where to find it, so I guess we just have to follow our instincts," Jake says.

"I agree. Where do you think Magdalene is now? Do you think she returned to Scotland after she…after?" Samir asks.

"Yes. I suspect she only traveled to Epsom to ambush us. The witches there don't know much about our plans, fortunately. Simha said he refused to give her any information so I suspect she is searching for answers, just like we are."

"Try and get some rest now. You look exhausted," Samir says. "I will wake you if my presence on the plane starts causing a problem."

Closing his eyes, Jake is immediately confronted by Alexandra's image. He replays the last night they were together.

He arrives at Alexandra's apartment at 5 pm. She thinks they are going to see *Darker Demons* followed by dinner downtown. He has other plans.

He knows her migraine medication makes her drowsy. He breaks up a couple of pills and dissolves them in wine. She is asleep within 15 minutes.

Shedding his human form he carries her down the stairs to his car. Driving to the building where he and Caitlin have set up the fake hospital room, he has a moment of doubt and considers taking her back to her apartment.

Realizing it is safer for her if he just goes through with the plan he drives to the building. Carrying her inside he briefly imagines they are somewhere else; somewhere far from New Orleans and Caitlin.

Caitlin and the two prostitutes she hired to watch Alexandra arrive minutes later. She orders Jake out of the room while she finishes preparing the scene.

Undressing Alexandra, she places her in a hospital gown and hooks up the IV. Filling it with the drug-filled mixture she paid a real hospital employee to provide, she inserts the needle into Alexandra's hand.

Alexandra groans. She seems to come around briefly before the medication takes effect and knocks her out. Instructing the two women on what is expected of them, she leaves to join Jake in the hallway.

"She's all set," Caitlin says. "Are you sure you don't want to just kill her now and get it over with?"

Annoyed at being questioned again, Jake tells her, "I'm sure. We're sticking to the plan."

Caitlin asks about the device Jake supposedly implanted in Alexandra's neck; the one that allows him to control her thoughts.

Lying, he tells her it is a device his company has been working on. He tells her it will earn him millions.

"Between that and what you'll inherit from the Judge, we'll be multi-millionaires," he tells Caitlin.

"How does it work?" she wants to know.

Pulling her close, he presses his mouth to her ear, "Come on babe, you know you don't understand the technical jargon," he whispers.

Things go as planned until somehow the IV needle is removed from Alexandra's hand and she wakes up.

He now suspects it was Lorelei who removed it. A sudden jolt awakens him. Afraid Samir has caused a malfunction, he is relieved to hear the pilot announcing they are about to land.

Once settled at their hotel, Jake pulls out his phone and dials Claire's number.

Sounding anxious, she answers immediately, wanting to know if he has found Alexandra.

"No, but I think we are close," he says. "I need you to do something for me, Claire."

"You know I can't refuse you," she reminds him.

"I know. I remember," he tells her, briefly visualizing Claire's naked form beneath him.

"So what is it you need?" she asks.

"I need you to convince Lucien I am in France. Tell him I have a lead and I'm going to Mont Saint Michel. I don't want him to know I am in Scotland," he says.

"Scotland? Ah, this is connected to Rosslyn Chapel then," she says.

Surprised, Jake says, "I didn't know it was, but, maybe…yes, it could be."

"Well I'm glad I could help," she says.

Haltingly, Jake tells her his other news. "Claire, Aaron is gone. Magdalene ambushed him. I wasn't there to protect him."

"I'm so sorry Jake. Don't blame yourself. I don't know what happened but I do know Magdalene has become very dangerous. Just take care of yourself, and find our girl," she tells him. "I will take care of Lucien."

CHAPTER 47

After ending the conversation with Jake, Claire summons Rosslyn to her office.

"I think you need to know what's happening," she tells Rosslyn.

"Is there some news about Alexandra?" Rosslyn asks, fearing the worst.

Shaking her head, Claire answers, "No, not yet. I just spoke to Jake. He and Samir, the wind wraith, are in Scotland. Jake's assistant, Aaron, is gone; killed by Magdalene. I knew him. He was decent and very loyal to Jake.

"Jake and I were…we knew each other many, many years ago. Back then, he was going by the name Jacques Saint Germaine. The night he showed up carrying Alexandra's body was the first time I had seen him in over 100 years but a demon's spell has no time limit. He has asked me for a favor and I can't refuse him. I wouldn't, even if I could.

"I'm telling you all this so you will understand why I am going to lie to Alexandra's father and why I may need your help."

Rosslyn reaches out her arms and Claire goes to her. "You know I will do whatever I can," she tells Claire.

"It could go badly if Lucien knows I am lying," she warns Rosslyn.

"We can handle him," she assures Claire.

Claire leaves her friend's soothing embrace and fetches her phone. While listening to the recorded message on Lucien's voicemail, Claire composes her story.

"Lucien, it's Claire. I have some news. I have heard from the demon. He is on his way to France, to Mont Saint Michel. Alexandra is with the witches of Racines. The demon claims the lock is somehow related to this area.

"Rosslyn and I will leave for Paris in the morning. I expect we will see you in Racines."

Turning to Rosslyn she says, "We better start making arrangements. I will call Celestine and tell her what is happening, in case Lucien arrives before we do. I will let Jake know what we are doing. Maybe we can delay Lucien long enough to give him a chance to find Alexandra.

"Why are you smiling?" Claire asks.

Rosslyn says, "I have always wanted to visit France."

"Well bear in mind this is not a pleasure trip," she scolds the younger witch. "Still, it would be nice to see Paris again," she adds, softly.

CHAPTER 48

Lucien is enjoying the company of a beautiful young woman when his phone interrupts. Checking the number, he decides Claire can wait. Turning to refocus his attention on his companion, he sees she is already out of bed and getting dressed.

"What's this? Why are you leaving so soon?" he demands to know.

"I have a job and I need to get back to it," she tells him. "It's been great, thanks!"

Leaping out of bed, he grabs her by the shoulders. "I am not ready for you to leave," he says.

Sounding alarmed, she says, "Listen. I'm sorry but I really have to go. Please let go of me."

Seeing the look of fear on her face, Lucien releases his hold. "Go then! You are not worth my time."

Hurriedly putting on the rest of her clothes, the girl rushes out the door.

"Stupid child," he spits out.

He picks up his phone and calls Claire. After several rings, she answers.

"I'll have you know, you just spoiled a lovely afternoon. What is it you want?" he asks.

"Didn't you even listen to my message?" she asks.

"I don't have time for that. Just tell me why you called," he says.

Claire repeats the story she had left on his voicemail.

"So, she is in France. Good. I will meet you there tomorrow, and Claire? I hope for your sake you are telling me the truth," he says.

CHAPTER 49

Alexandra awakens. Sensing a presence in the room, she tries to gauge the intruder's intentions. The form appears to be that of a tall man. As she stares, the features become clear. It's Tom.

"Get out Alex! Hurry!" she hears her friend cry out.

Then a horrible gurgling sound comes from his throat.

Having only seconds to react, Alexandra closes her eyes and focuses her mind on New Orleans. Picturing herself safely within the walls of her old home, she feels her spirit moving through time and space. Cloaking her mind from Magdalene, she barely escapes capture.

Opening her eyes, she sees the familiar walls of the bedroom in which she spent her childhood. Shaken, she opens the door and calls for her friend Rosslyn. The witch who answers is not Rosslyn but Elena.

Stunned by the sudden appearance of Alexandra, Elena asks, "What…how, what are you doing here?"

"I was almost caught by Magdalene. I needed to escape in a hurry and this felt like the safest place to run," she explains. "I need to see Rosslyn."

"I'm sorry but she's not here. Neither is Claire," Elena tells her.

"Why? Where are they?" Alexandra asks, not understanding why her two friends would have left their home.

"They're out looking for you," Elena tells her. Elena explains Rosslyn and Claire have left for France.

"They think you are in the convenhome in Racines," she says.

Perplexed, Alexandra asks why they think she is in France.

"I'm afraid I don't know the answer to that. They simply said they were going to France and they are supposed to meet with Lucien when they arrive."

Suspecting they have purposely misled her father, Alexandra ends her questioning of Elena.

"Thank you, Elena. Please don't tell anyone I am here, and if you could help cloak my presence, I would appreciate it," she tells her.

"Of course. I'll do everything I can to help," Elena replies.

Returning to her bedroom, Alexandra wonders how Magdalene could have found her. She is sure none of the witches in Cádiz are responsible.

"How was she able to track me down?" she wonders.

Sitting down on the bed, she finds her phone is still on the night table where Claire had left it after calling Jake. Picking it up, she sees the last number called was his. Her heart flutters at the sight of his face on the screen.

Aching to hear his voice, she wonders how much she would put both of them at risk if she called.

Unable to resist, she pushes the button and listens as the call connects and his phone begins to ring.

On the other side of the ocean, Jake picks up his phone and sees her name on the caller ID. Not expecting it to really be Alexandra he answers anyway.

"Hello?" he says.

Gasping as her heart is gripped by a cold fist, she answers. "Jake, is it really you?"

"Alexandra?"

"Yes Jake, it's me. I miss you so much. I just needed to hear your voice. I love you," she says, the words pouring out as she exhales.

Jake answers "I love you too," saying the words for the first time in his long existence.

"I can't stay on the line. I'm afraid it could lead Magdalene right to you. She almost caught me in Cádiz."

Hearing Jake's sharp intake of breath, she quickly adds, "Don't worry. I won't let my guard down again. Where are you?" she asks.

"Scotland," he tells her. "Are you coming here?" he asks.

"Yes," she says before she hangs up.

CHAPTER 50

Infuriated at the loss of Alexandra, Magdalene needs to release her anger somewhere. The witches at Cádiz are too powerful for her. She decides to revisit Azurine.

The young witch is sleeping when Magdalene enters her room. She is abruptly awakened by Magdalene throwing off her covers and climbing on top of her.

Cruelly using Azurine to vent her frustration, she eventually exhausts herself and rolls over onto her side. Grabbing Azurine's hair, she twists the young witch's head until they are face to face. Magdalene sees tears streaming down Azurine's face.

"What's wrong with you? Why are you crying?" she asks, harshly.

Instead of answering, Azurine jumps out of bed grabs her clothes and runs out into the hall. Racing towards Esmeralda's room, she hears Magdalene behind her. Grabbing Azurine's shoulders, she spins the young witch around to face her.

"What do you think you're doing?" she asks.

Panicking, Azurine screams at Magdalene to leave her alone. The noise awakens Esmeralda and the other witches in the covenhome. They stream into the hallway wanting to know what is happening.

Realizing she is outnumbered, Magdalene escapes back to Scotland in a rush of foul wind.

Finally admitting to herself she needs help finding and taking Alexandra, Magdalene makes a call to Lucien. He answers the phone with a question.

"Who is this?"

"Lucien, it's Magdalene," she says.

There is a lengthy pause on the other end, prompting Magdalene to ask if Lucien is still there.

"Yes…yes, I am here. So it's true. You are possessing Alexandra's young man," Lucien states.

Laughing, Magdalene replies, "Her young man? No, Lucien. A man? Yes."

"Did you call to play word games with me?" Lucien asks.

"No. I called to ask for your help," Magdalene answers.

Making a disgusted sound, Lucien asks why he should help her when she has tried to murder his daughter.

"Because my love, you will need my help to find her," Magdalene says.

Informing her he knows where Alexandra is, he tells Magdalene she has nothing to offer him. "I am headed for France tomorrow to fetch her," he says.

"Ah, someone has misinformed you. Alexandra is not in France. She was in Cádiz until a short time ago," she says. "Now, I'm not sure where she is."

Lucien tells her he does not believe her story. "My source is very reliable," he says. "Besides, if you admit you don't know where she is, then how do you know she is not in France?"

"Fine, then go on to France. When you discover I am telling you the truth, call me," Magdalene says and hangs up.

She crawls into bed and is instantly asleep. Tom, however, is still awake.

CHAPTER 51

Claire and Rosslyn arrive at the Charles de Gaulle Airport and after clearing customs, head for Racines. Rosslyn anxiously asks Claire when they will be visiting Paris.

"When we have finished our business, maybe we can spend a little time in the city," Claire tells her.

"What exactly is our business?" Rosslyn asks.

Claire explains to Rosslyn she has spoken to Celestine and they have devised a way they hope will keep Lucien occupied for a few days. She tells Rosslyn there are ruins of an ancient abbey not far from Racines.

"The Savigny Abbey ruins are not visited by many tourists," she explains to Rosslyn. "We believe if we can lure Lucien to the site, we can hold him there. It will take the two of us and most of the witches in Racines, but, we will attempt to form a binding circle. Celestine and I believe the magic of the site itself will help us."

Rosslyn asks, "What happens after a few days when we let him go? Won't there be consequences?"

Nodding, Claire tells her friend, "If we let him go and the gateway is open, there will not be much Lucien can do. If that does not happen, or, if he finds a way to escape…I could be leading you to your doom."

Reaching over to take Claire's hand, Rosslyn assures her she is not worried. "Whatever happens, I made the decision to come on my own. You didn't force me. And if anything happened to you…I can't even think about it."

"Let us hope we will return to share a bottle of Chateau Margaux at a small Parisienne cafe before the week is over," Claire says, squeezing Rosslyn's hand.

CHAPTER 52

Still in shock, Jake turns to Samir. "It was Alexandra," he says, staring down at the phone, mesmerized. He is afraid if he moves he will awaken and discover the call was only a dream.

"You are not asleep my friend," Samir assures him. "What did she say?"

Jake turns his gaze towards Samir, answering, "Not very much. She was in Cádiz but Magdalene found her. She barely escaped. She said she is coming to Scotland."

"That is good news," Samir says.

"Yes, it is," Jake agrees. "I don't know when she is coming. I guess we'll just have to wait and trust she will know how to find us."

Samir nods in agreement. "While we are waiting, why don't we pay a visit to Rosslyn Chapel. You said Claire thought all of this might have some connection to the chapel."

Jake agrees it would be a good idea to visit the place. He has been reading up on the history since Claire spoke about a possible connection to the gateway but hasn't uncovered anything. Knowing the area was home to one of the first covens, he believes that could be the thread binding it all together.

He asks Samir, "Have you ever visited the chapel?"

The wind wraith replies he has not. He adds it is a place he has always wanted to see.

"A place that is the source of so many tales and legends must have magick surrounding it. Have you ever been there?" he asks Jake.

Shaking his head, he tells Samir he hasn't been to the site either. "It's funny. Aaron used to talk about visiting. He said it 'spoke' to him. I don't know if he meant it literally, but he could have."

They decide to leave immediately in order to get to the chapel before closing time. Walking through the quiet Scottish countryside, Jake finds it easy to imagine what the area was like when the first Anantan arrived. It is still a wild land in spite of human attempts to pave it over and tame it. The herbal aroma of heather is everywhere combined with the salty smell of the North Sea.

Picturing Alexandra beside him, her long raven hair blowing in the wind, Jake feels his chest tighten.

"I wonder if Claire has managed to sidetrack Lucien," Samir says, pulling Jake out of his reverie.

"If she hadn't, I think we would have heard something by now," Jake answers.

Approaching their destination, Jake begins to feel an odd tingling sensation coming up from the ground. It feels like electricity entering through his feet and pulsing through his body. Looking around, he doesn't see any rain clouds. He doesn't hear thunder or see lightning.

Turning to Samir, he opens his mouth to tell his friend what's happening but doesn't get the chance. The roots of the wych elm tree beside the road reach up and pull him under.

Jake feels himself falling. All he can see on his descent is an odd green light coming from everywhere and nowhere. He hits the bottom with a jolt that makes his teeth rattle. Turning a full 360 degrees, he observes he is in a vast open space with tunnels branching off in many directions.

Calling out he asks, "Is anyone…is anything here?"

He hears a sound behind him and recognizes the birdsong that is Samir when he becomes the wind.

Relieved to not be alone, he asks Samir if he has any idea where they are.

"I'm not sure. I saw you disappear and followed the sound of your voice," Samir tells him

Puzzled, Jake asks, "My voice? I didn't think I said anything on the way down."

"It was more of a shout than actual words," Samir replies, trying not to embarrass Jake.

"Ah…that makes sense. It was a bit disconcerting to be kidnapped by a tree," Jake tells him.

Deciding they should explore, they head for the north tunnel; the one leading towards the chapel. They don't come across any other creatures, alive or dead. The walls radiate the same green light Jake saw on his way down. There is a strong aroma of earth and something sweet they can't identify.

Stopping, Jake says, "I recognize that smell. It's the Pratika flower, from Privthi. Simha had the blooms in his shop. This must mean we are close to the original covenhome."

As they continue walking, they see writing on the walls of the tunnel; alien symbols neither can decipher. The aroma of the Pratika grows stronger. Jake feels heaviness in his limbs. He finds it hard to keep walking. Even Samir is not immune to the magick. The two stop and drop to the ground in a stupor.

CHAPTER 53

Lucien arrives in Paris feeling out of sorts. The flight was crowded; even in first class. There was turbulence over the ocean. The food served was colorless, as was the stewardess.

After clearing customs, he marches over to the car rental counter to pick up his reserved Jaguar. The woman at the car counter, unlike the stewardess, is young and vivacious. Smiling at Lucien, she breezes through the paperwork and gives him directions to the vehicle.

"Will you be staying in Paris tonight?" she asks.

Sadly shaking his head, he tells her, "No, I must meet some friends in Racines. Perhaps I will be in Paris in a few days. Will you give me your number?"

Touching his hand, she leans over the counter and tucks a card with her number on it into his front pocket.

Inhaling her Patchouli scent arouses him. He takes her hand and kisses it, promising to call if he is staying in Paris.

Driving to Racines, Lucien plans how he will approach his daughter. He suspects Lorelei warned her to beware of him; that he might not have Alexandra's best interests at heart. In fact, he loves his daughter and would not intentionally cause her pain. Unfortunately, his actions could have unintended consequences.

Wondering where the demon is and why he has not received a return phone call, he acknowledges to himself Eziel might suspect his intentions are not entirely pure. If that is the case, he thinks, the demon will make every effort to thwart his plans.

The rhythm of the road eventually lulls Lucien into a peaceful state of mind. Enjoying the passing scenes of the French countryside, he thinks it might be time to relocate.

"I've been in New Orleans for centuries. A new environment might be the perfect thing for me," he thinks.

The ringing phone interrupts his reverie. It's Claire. He pushes the button on the steering wheel to answer and engages the auto drive.

"Hello, Claire. Where are you?" he asks.

"I'm here in Racines, waiting for you. Where are you?" she wants to know.

"I am almost there. Is Alexandra with you?" he asks.

Claire tells him she is staying at the covenhome, but she is not available to speak with him.

"She's in the meditation chamber," she tells Lucien.

"Does she know I am coming?" Lucien asks.

Debating which way to go with her lie, Claire decides to tell Lucien his daughter does not know he is on his way.

"We all thought it was best not to tell her," she says.

Laughing, Lucien asks, "Are you afraid she will run away?"

"Honestly, yes," Claire tells him.

Lucien demands to know the details of Claire's plan.

"How do you plan on preventing Alexandra's disappearance the moment she sees me?"

Breathing deeply, Claire carefully lays out the trap she has set for Lucien, knowing one slip could send him racing away.

"We think the meeting should take place at the Savigny Abbey ruins. The witches of Racines have

agreed to help us form a binding circle to keep
Alexandra from escaping. Once you have had the
opportunity to speak to her, we will allow her to decide
whether she wants to go with you or remain at Racines."

Feeling a slight tremor of apprehension, Lucien
asks, "Will you be meeting me there, are shall we go
together?"

"Rosslyn, you and I will travel there together once
the witches have taken Alexandra and formed their
circle," she answers, hoping he does not detect the
trembling in her voice.

"Very well, I will see you soon," he tells her. He
spends the rest of the drive trying to find Alexandra, to
confirm she is indeed in Racines, but Lorelei's veil is
still strong. He cannot detect whether she is close or
very far away.

Seeing storm clouds ahead, Lucien speeds up,
hoping to beat the rain. He is unsuccessful and gets to
the convenhome later than expected and in a worse
temper than when he arrived in Paris. Claire sees him
drive up and rushes out to meet him.

"Lucien, we are running late. We should leave
immediately," she tells him.

Angrily, he asks where Rosslyn is. "If you are in
such a hurry, why isn't she out here with you?"

Turning towards the building, Claire shouts for
Rosslyn to hurry and join them.

"She just stopped to grab a coat," Claire tells him.
Rosslyn rushes out the door and the three are on their
way to the ruins before Lucien has an opportunity to ask
any more questions. It is a very short drive to the site.

Arriving at the ruins, Lucien begins to have doubts.
He feels Claire and Rosslyn are nervous and distracted.

Pausing to scan the area, Lucien doesn't see anyone else; no witches and no Alexandra.

Taking his hand, Claire leads him towards the area where the circle has been created. Lucien sees the markings on the ground, the familiar symbols, and assumes they are for Alexandra.

Entering the circle, he immediately realizes his mistake. The witches materialize all around him. He is trapped in the center, alone.

Glaring at her, Lucien says, "I am surprised at you Claire. You know what will happen once I am released from this trap. Enjoy your last days of existence."

Before walking away she tells him, "We will return when the gateway is reopened and maybe we will let you go if you promise to behave."

The witches finish spinning the web which will be Lucien's prison. Claire understands if things go badly and Lucien escapes, she truly could have only a few more days to live. Turning to Rosslyn, she takes her hand and they leave the ruins together without a backward glance.

CHAPTER 54

Jake and Samir awaken to find themselves in a large room. Something has moved them from the spot where they lost consciousness, but they do not have any company in the chamber. There is a circular mark on the floor surrounding a beam of light. Markings on the walls accompany beautiful drawings depicting the witches who had once lived there.

There are drawings of ceremonies and feasts; scenes of daily life. It is a priceless chronicle of early Anantan life. Spellbound, the two take it all in, moving from one exquisite scene to another.

Hearing a sound emanating from within the beam of light, they turn towards it. They see the form of a witch materialize in the center. The apparition begins to speak.

"I am Rowena, one of the explorers. We have built our convenhome here. We have brought with us the knowledge you will one day need to reopen the gateway and journey home. If you are here, you know part of the answer. Bring the key to this spot and you will find the rest."

The vision disappears and with it the beam of light. Frustrated at the lack of information, Jake shouts at the vanished witch, "We don't know part of the answer. We don't know anything!"

Samir reminds him they know Alexandra is the key and now they know the lock is somewhere in Roslin.

"I feel the chapel will play a part in the final solution, "Samir says. "We should return to the surface and continue our trip."

"Do you have any idea how we get back to the surface?" Jake asks.

Pointing to one of the paintings, Samir says, "I think our directions are right there."

The two study the images and see they are in fact a map of the covenhome. The tunnel leading to the surface is off to the left.

Once above ground again, Jake and Samir continue their walk to Rosslyn Chapel. Approaching the building, Jake senses a presence, a familiar one. Turning around, he sees Alexandra. Rushing towards her, he reaches out his arms but before he can reach her, she disappears.

Turning to his friend, he asks, "What happened? What the hell just happened?"

Samir answers he doesn't know but suspects Alexandra's mind was reaching out, searching for Jake.

"Now she knows where you are, she will come," he tells his friend.

The two continue on as the late afternoon sun sets the face of the chapel on fire. Inside, the multitude of intricate carvings covering every surface create the sensation of entering a three-dimensional sculpture. Subtle vibrations emanating from the stones have a dizzying effect on Jake. He reaches out to steady himself on the closest column. Realizing his mistake as the column comes alive with color, changing and shifting like a kaleidoscope, he quickly pulls his hand back.

He looks towards Samir to see if his friend noticed the peculiar effect. His friend doesn't appear to have been paying any attention. Samir's expression is blissful. Head cocked to one side, he seems to be listening to a symphony for one.

Tapping Samir's shoulder, Jake asks what it is he is hearing.

"The music of the stones, of life, of all creation," Samir answers. "It is present here in a way I have never experienced before. "

Shaking his head, Jake says, "I can't hear anything out of the ordinary, but..." He places his hand back on the column to show Samir the effect. "What do you make of that?" he asks.

Samir sees someone approaching and tells Jake to pull his hand away, saying, "We are attracting unwanted attention."

The man introduces himself as a guide and asks if the two have any questions about the chapel.

Nodding, Samir tells him, "I have heard a musical score was discovered encoded in the stones. Is that true?"

"Yes, it is true. We have recordings in the gift shop if you are interested," the guide tells him, hoping to entice the two to leave. He feels uncomfortable in their presence, getting the sense they are communicating with the carvings.

Hearing his thoughts, Samir says, "Don't worry. We are going to be leaving shortly."

"How did you...I wasn't suggesting you leave. Please forgive me if it seemed like that. It's just...we are closing in 15 minutes," the guide stammers.

Jake tells the guide they will be gone in five. He doesn't want to admit to Samir he finds the building disturbing. They walk hurriedly away, trying to cover as much ground as they can before closing time.

CHAPTER 55

Alexandra's consciousness is reaching out searching for Jake. Finally locating him, she can see he is standing in front of Rosslyn Chapel. He senses her presence and looks towards her; rushes to meet her, not realizing she is only a projection. She can't understand why he is with Gregory's wind wraith, Samir.

Seeing Jake again leaves her shaken; trembling violently. Alexandra's last honest memory of him is from the night of the murder; the night Jake and Caitlin had kidnapped her. She is aware in the days after, he had saved her life and cleared her name, but that has not erased the wound of his betrayal.

Feeling love and hate in equal measure, her desire for him outweighs both. Her body is raw. The slightest touch of a breeze ignites her like flame on kindling. Closing her eyes, she conjures up visions of his naked body so real her fingertips throb in time with his heartbeat.

She hears Elena's voice calling, reaching down into the deep well of her fantasy and pulling her out.

"Alexandra! Wake up! You need to go. Magdalene has found you. I don't know how. I tried to cloak your presence but she was able to see through it. We feel her spirit. She is almost here."

Painfully banishing the vision of Jake, Alexandra collects herself and answers Elena.

"Thank you for trying. Please just protect yourselves. I will be fine," she tells her as they share a parting embrace.

She wonders if that is true. "Will I be fine or am I headed for my demise?"

Believing it is safe to return to Cádiz, she summons up a vision of the room with the red curtains. Opening her eyes, she sees the familiar surroundings. She races to the gathering room, hoping the witches will all be there.

She finds Dawn and Oleander, but no others.

"What has happened?" she asks, not really wanting to hear the answer.

Wearily lifting her head, Dawn's face brightens when she sees Alexandra.

"Thank goodness…we thought you were lost to us," she says, rushing to Alexandra; wrapping her arms around the witch she had feared was dead.

"Magdalene has been here. She is more powerful than we realized. She sent three of our sisters to the Akashic Realm. The rest are in hiding, attempting to regain their strength."

Heartbroken, Alexandra tells her, "This is my fault. I am so sorry. I will finish this alone. I will leave for Scotland immediately."

Holding her, Dawn says, "It is not your fault and you will do no such thing. We are going to Scotland together, the three of us."

Alexandra turns to Oleander, asking, "Is this true? Do you want to risk your life for this?"

The witch answers, saying, "This is not your quest alone, Alexandra. This concerns all who are trapped here; all those who wish to come here, but find the path blocked. We need to put an end to it, to reopen the gateways. It is the hour and we are the chosen."

"Oleander is right. It is time," Alexandra says.

CHAPTER 56

Magdalene has chased Alexandra from Cádiz to New Orleans growing more desperate with each thwarted attempt to capture the witch. Expecting to at least find Claire in New Orleans, she is instead confronted by a group of young, inexperienced witches. She is too tired to bother with them and simply leaves them with a warning, saying, "If I find out you are hiding Alexandra, I will return and I will not be pleased!"

Debating whether to return to Scotland or head to France to find Lucien, she chooses France.

Acknowledging she is unable to catch Alexandra off guard, she hopes to enlist his help. Not knowing exactly where Lucien is, Magdalene heads for the covenhome in Marseille.

The witches greet her in a non-committal manner.

They are not friendly, nor do they send her away. She asks to speak to the head of the group and is taken to a witch named Tentarice. Magdalene is entranced by the witch's beauty making it difficult for her to answer when asked, "Why have you come to Marseille, monsieur?"

Stumbling over the words, Magdalene answers, "I am…I was…I had heard the witches in Marseille surpass all others in beauty. I must say, I find this to be true."

Frowning, Tentarice replies, "Please do not waste your false flattery on me. I see your heart is dark and I demand to know what it is you are after."

Flustered, Magdalene tries again, "Please, it is not false flattery. You are beautiful beyond any other. I only wished for a chance to gaze upon such beauty."

In spite of herself, Tentarice is flattered by Magdalene's words.

"Very well. You have been given that opportunity, now you may go."

Magdalene replies, "While that is true, spending a few hours in your company would allow me to die a happy man."

"Perhaps death is what you are after," Tentarice answers, "Since you refuse to obey my words and leave me in peace."

Magdalene senses she is winning the witch over and says, "Leaving you in peace would leave me brokenhearted. Let us at least share a glass of wine and I will leave immediately after."

Tentarice is uncertain. She is tempted by the handsome man she sees standing before her, yet she senses a duality, a darkness inside of him.

Finally making up her mind, she nods her head slightly and tells Magdalene, "Just one glass, then I must insist you go."

Smiling, Magdalene holds out her hand and Tentarice accepts it. The two stroll down to the waterfront and find a small restaurant with a view of the harbor.

Once seated, Magdalene takes Tentarice's hand and lifts it to her lips. Kissing each finger as she stares into the witch's eyes, her will weakens. Tom senses an opportunity and reasserts himself.

"She is lying to you. The witch Magdalene is in possession of my body. She's looking for Alexandra. She…" Tom doesn't get the chance to finish.

Tentarice leaps up from her chair and orders Magdalene to leave.

"Leave me and leave Marseille now!" she commands.

In a fury, Magdalene reaches out and grabs the witch's hair. Pulling a knife out of her pocket, she is about to plunge it into her heart, when Tom stops her. Struggling to get his spirit under control, she is too weak to hold on to Tentarice. She lets go and Tentarice immediately makes her escape.

People are shouting at the waitress to call the police. Some are getting up from their chairs and heading towards Magdalene. Closing her eyes, she wills herself to Scotland. Exhausted, she collapses on the bed and falls deeply into sleep.

CHAPTER 57

Returning to their hotel, Jake and Samir are unaware of Magdalene's proximity. They plan on meeting for dinner after they have had time to rest and process the events of the day.

Jake's recently acquired emotions are churning his insides, turning them from steel to butter. Remembering Alexandra's spectral image, he aches to touch her. His fingers remember the texture of her skin; his mouth still tastes her lips. His love for her is a sudden downpour in a dessert, filling the space inside him he hadn't realized was empty.

Closing his eyes, he remembers times they were together when he should have been savoring every ounce of her; instead, he had simply taken her presence for granted. The memory of his affair with Caitlin sits coldly on his heart.

He falls asleep and dreams of Alexandra. They are together in a room with red curtains. He hears the sound of the sea outside. Holding her, he feels complete. She turns her head to look up at him. Her lips are moving but he doesn't understand what she is saying.

"Wake up Jake!" Samir says again, shaking his shoulder.

Groggily, Jake opens his eyes, "What? Did something happen?'

"No. It's just time for dinner," Samir tells him.

The short walk to the restaurant gives Jake little time to shake off his dream. Samir notes the preoccupied expression on Jake's face.

"You seem to be somewhere far away," he tells his friend.

Grinning, Jake answers, "I was dreaming about Alexandra when you woke me up. We were someplace warm, in a room by the ocean. I didn't recognize it."

Samir answers, "Let's hope it was a premonition."

Sighing heavily Jake says, "I have a feeling we will get the answers to all of our questions soon. Whether they are the ones we want remains to be seen."

CHAPTER 58

Alexandra and the two witches of Cádiz board the plane to Scotland. Turning to Dawn, Alexandra asks, "Remind me. Why are we traveling this way?"

Patting her hand, Dawn answers, "It's the safest and least taxing way to travel. Every time we will ourselves through time and space, it creates a ripple which can be detected by others of our kind. This way, we are cloaked, and besides, it is much more relaxing."

"Relaxing for you maybe," Alexandra replies. "I hate it."

"Just think about your demon. You should be with him soon," Dawn says.

Closing her eyes, Alexandra does just that. She sees herself in the room with red curtains. Jake is with her. He has his arms around her; her head rests gently on his chest. Stroking her hair, he whispers how much he loves her. Saying he could never live without her, he lifts her chin and lowers his lips to hers.

She turns her back to him, exposing her scar. He runs his tongue over the crenulated flesh that tastes of burning hot stones. His teeth gently pierce the skin feeding on the current of life running through her.

Gasping, she feels a sudden jolt and awakens to find the plane is flying through a thunderstorm.

Trembling from the remnants of the dream and the sudden fear of the lurching plane, Alexandra asks, "How much longer?"

"We are almost there," Dawn tells her. "Don't worry. This is just a little bad weather. We'll pass through it shortly."

Regaining her equilibrium, Alexandra says, "We should plan what we are going to do when we arrive in Scotland."

Leaning over Dawn, Oleander says, "It is really up to you. You are the key. The decision is yours."

"When we arrive, it will be late. We should just stay in Edinburgh. First thing tomorrow we will head to Rosslyn Chapel. I believe Jake will look for us there. The book suggested the lock could be found there as well. I feel Magdalene is in Scotland. She will be expecting us too."

Dawn asks, "Will you recognize her?"

Nodding sadly, Alexandra answers, "Yes. She has taken the form of a dear friend of mine. It breaks my heart to think of what has to be done to stop her."

Oleander says, "We are sorry for that but, she has already taken several souls whom we loved."

Alexandra answers, "I know and I still blame myself for all of this."

Dawn shakes her head, telling Alexandra, "The only fault rests with the witch Eve who tried to take a human through the gateway. She robbed us all of our freedom. Now, it is almost over."

"What if I fail?" Alexandra asks. "There is no guarantee we will solve the riddle and find the lock, and even if we do, Magdalene, or Lucien, or someone else, could stop us."

Dawn says, "We will succeed. I have faith in you."

Another lightning bolt sizzles outside the window of the plane as it dips and rises like a roller coaster.

Attempting to distract herself, Alexandra tells Dawn she doesn't quite understand why controlling the gateway is so important to so many.

"What is it they hope to gain?" she asks.

Dawn explains, "Imagine having the ability to travel anywhere in the universe in a few seconds. Imagine you are the only one in this world who has this gift. You could journey to any world amassing untold wealth.

"You could use your fortune to build an army and rule the world. The earth would belong to you."

"But once the passages are open, won't others want to come to earth, the way they once did?" Alexandra asks.

"Yes, I expect they will. But, there are ways to close the portals. If you closed all but one and kept that securely guarded, you could keep others out," Dawn explains.

Oleander joins the conversation saying, "And, imagine the chaos if…when all of the gateways are reopened at once. Humans will panic. They won't understand what is happening. Everything they believe in; their gods, their governments, their truths; all will be torn away.

"If you have control of the passages, you can gain control of humanity. They will follow anyone who makes them feel safe again, who can provide them with answers."

"I see. So what happens if I am the one who is supposed to have the answers, and I have none?" Alexandra asks.

CHAPTER 59

Claire and Rosslyn board a plane bound for
Scotland, leaving the witches of Racines to guard
Lucien. Claire knows if he manages to escape, he will
come after both of them. She also knows if they succeed
in keeping him captive until the gateway is open, he will
accept the outcome and leave them alone.

"How will we find Alexandra once we are in
Scotland?" Rosslyn asks.

Claire answers, "Lorelei's veil has grown weaker. I
believe she must have passed over. Once we are closer
to Alexandra, I should be able to locate her…at least I
hope so. Time is growing very short now."

Without warning, Rosslyn asks, "Did you and
Lucien ever have an affair?"

Laughing, Claire answers, "No, Rosslyn, we never
did. What would make you ask that?"

"I don't know. It just occurred to me you understand
him very well, like someone you have been intimate
with," Rosslyn answers.

Claire shakes her head and tells the younger witch,
"We have known each other for a very long time. I was
close to Lorelei. That's all. He left Alexandra in my care
because of our friendship. He knew I would love her as I
would my own child."

Smiling, Rosslyn answers, "We all love her."

"I know you do. Now Eziel, that's another story!"
Claire says, shaking her head and laughing.

Rosslyn says, "Tell me about him. What was it like
to have a demon lover?"

Claire says, "It was…I don't know if I have the right
words to describe it. He was so handsome he made my

eyes ache. Looking at him was like drinking too much wine; it was dizzying. He was charming and funny, and when I was with him he made me feel like there was no one else alive."

Sighing, Rosslyn says, "Why didn't you stay with him?"

"You don't 'stay with' a demon. I knew that from the beginning. I think it made the whole episode even more exciting! Now, with Alexandra, things are different. He has fallen in love with her. Once a demon falls in love, he is bound forever," Claire says.

Rosslyn asks, "Do you think they will return to Privthi if the gateway is reopened?"

"You mean when it is reopened; when they are all reopened," Claire answers. "I don't know. Who can say what any of us will do? The gateways will transform the world. All of the Anantan, as well as the humans, will be able to travel to other realms. Tomorrow will not be like today."

"I can't imagine it," Rosslyn says.

Claire tells her, "Get some rest now. There is still much that needs to be done."

CHAPTER 60

Hearing someone knocking on her door, Alexandra groggily gets up from the bed. She doesn't check to see who it is; just throws open the door. The sight of Tom standing there befuddles her.

"Where am I? What's going on?" she asks.

As the truth slowly sinks in, she gasps and tries to slam the door, but Tom's hand shoots out and blocks her. The other hand is holding a long knife which he swings in a wide arc ending with Alexandra's neck.

She wakes up screaming. There is someone knocking on her door. Cautiously she approaches and looks out the peephole. What she sees on the other side fills her with relief and joy. Opening the door she reaches out and embraces her old friend.

Rosslyn returns the hug, then holding her at arm's length, says, "We heard a scream. What on earth happened? I was terrified!"

"I was having a horrible nightmare. Magdalene found me, and cut off my head," Alexandra answers, shuddering. "I am so happy to see you, but, how did you find me?"

"If you let us in, I will tell you," Claire says.

Alexandra gives Claire a hug and says, "Of course. I'm so sorry. I'm still half asleep. Please come in and sit down."

Intently staring at Alexandra, Claire asks, "Is everything all right? Has your wound healed properly?"

Nodding, Alexandra replies, "Yes, I'm fine; healthier than ever. Cádiz was good for my body and soul. I spoke with my mother. It was too short, but, at least I finally got the chance to see her. She was so beautiful."

Claire nods in agreement. "Yes, she was. I'm so happy to hear you had the opportunity to spend some time with her. It must have been hard for the two of you to say goodbye."

"It was but I understood why she had to go," Alexandra tells her.

"There were a couple of times after she left that Magdalene almost caught me, but, I managed to escape. I believe she is here in Scotland. I sense her presence."

Claire nods in agreement, saying, "Yes, we are certain she is here. Your father, by the way, is in France."

Alexandra tells Claire she suspected that was the case.

"When Elena told me where you and Rossy had gone, I thought you must have lured him there somehow."

Smiling, Claire answers, "Yes, we told him you were in Racines. We took him to the ruins at Savigny Abbey and the witches helped us contain him there. It was Jake who asked me to detain him. Hopefully, he will stay put until this is over."

"Jake is here as well," Alexandra says.

Nodding, Claire tells her, "Yes, it was Jake who told us you were in Scotland. Once we were here, it was just a matter of following the path you made in the atmosphere."

"Why did you trust Jake enough to betray my father?"

"Jake asked me to help him and I couldn't refuse."

Alexandra's eyes widen as Claire's simple statement reveals the truth, she had once been Jake's lover.

"You and Jake?" she asks.

Flustered, Claire answers, "Yes. It was many, many years ago, long before you were born."

"It's all right, I understand," Alexandra says. "It's nice to have someone who knows what it's like to be with him; to be under his spell."

Claire says, "Don't dismiss your feelings for him as just being under his spell. I believe you truly love each other. And really, isn't all love just being under a spell; seeing your beloved through a distorted lens? At least with Jake, you know exactly what you are getting."

Alexandra turns away and answers, "Yes. I'm getting a creature living only to enthrall others. Who knows how many lovers he has had; how many more he will have?"

Claire tells her, "The first question I can't answer but the second I can. He will only have one lover, one love, for the rest of his life. He is bound to you, as you are to him."

Sighing, Alexandra tells her, "When this is all over if we are still here, I will think about all of that. Right now, we need to figure out what our next move is. We still don't know who or what the lock is or even where to begin to look for answers."

A knock on the door startles everyone. Alexandra checks the peephole and sees it is Dawn and Oleander.

Opening the door, she says, "Please come in and join us."

After introducing everyone, Alexandra tells the new arrivals, "We were just discussing what to do next."

CHAPTER 61

Unable to sleep, Jake spends the night roaming the countryside surrounding Roslin. He senses Alexandra's nearness. The air is full of strange vibrations. There is a gathering of energy, unlike anything he has felt before.

Returning to the hotel, he finds Samir still sleeping.

"Wake up my friend," he says. "The finale of our play is about to begin."

Rubbing the sleep out of his eyes, Samir says, "You seem to be in fine spirits this morning. Did you sleep well?"

"Not at all, actually," Jake replies. "I am simply relieved this will all be over soon; for better or worse."

Samir agrees. "It will be an extraordinary day no matter what occurs."

They head for the dining room to have breakfast; the last moment of peace before the storm breaks.

Scanning the faces of his fellow diners, Jake wonders how they would react if they knew their world was about to change forever. Would they be afraid, he wonders.

Turning to Samir, he asks, "If we are successful in reopening the gateways, how do you think the humans will behave? Will they try and spin this into some sort of religious event? Will there be violence, upheaval?"

Samir takes a few seconds to consider Jake's question. Finally, shaking his head, he says, "I don't know the answer to that. I suspect some will say God is responsible; whoever and whatever they consider God to be. Others will take it as proof there is no God. Many will try and find a way to profit from the gateways. A few enlightened ones may seize the opportunity to travel the cosmos and learn all they can.

"One thing is certain. They will need someone to guide them; to explain what has happened and what it means. The Anantan will no longer be able to hide. Their days of anonymity will be over."

Jake asks, "What can that mean for me? Demons aren't very popular with humans."

"I think you're wrong about that," Samir replies. "Look at all of the books, movies and television shows they create about you!"

Jake smiles and shakes his head, "In the abstract, they like us. In reality, I think it will be a different story."

"You know you can travel through the gateway to Privthi, or anywhere you desire."

"I know," Jake says. "I am more worried about Alexandra. If she is the chosen one, does that mean it is her duty to lead us all through this transition?"

Samir answers, "Again, I do not know. The only way to find the answers is to go forward.

"I am a creature of this world. I could have traveled to other realms before the gateways closed but I chose to remain here. Now, I am ready to see the wonders beyond this place. I think the humans may surprise us both. Maybe they are ready too.

"But that is all in the future. For now, we need to focus on today."

Jake nods and says, "Yes. I believe Claire was right about all of this having a connection to Rosslyn Chapel. Magdalene may know that as well. I know she is close by. I doubt we will get through the day without a confrontation."

CHAPTER 62

The five witches are seated in a circle discussing their plans when there is yet another knock on the door. Alexandra looks through the peephole but doesn't recognize the face on the other side.

She asks, "May I help you?"

"Yes, Alexandra. My name is Esmeralda. I have come to help you," the face replies.

Alexandra hears Claire gasp at the name. Turning to Claire she asks, "Do you know her?"

"If it is the same Esmeralda, yes, I know her very well," Claire answers. She approaches the door and looks out. Recognizing her old friend, she throws open the door and reaches out her arms.

Esmeralda embraces Claire, saying, "I can hardly believe it, Claire! It has been centuries since I last saw you."

The two enter the room and Esmeralda joins the circle. After introducing everyone, Claire explains, "I met Esmeralda in Spain many, many centuries ago. She was one of the first arrivals from Privthi. She taught me many things. She was there when I reached my sexual awakening. I will never forget those days."

Alexandra asks, "How did you find us?"

"Your presence here has created ripples in the vātāvaran. It was not hard for me to follow them to their source."

Concerned, Alexandra asks, "Will it be that simple for others to find me?"

Shaking her head, Esmeralda replies, "That is doubtful. Most don't have my powers. However, if you are worried about Magdalene, I am afraid she may be strong enough."

Alexandra asks, "How do you know of Magdalene?"

Esmeralda tells her, "She came to my coven asking about you. She was using the body of a human male, a very handsome one. We told her honestly, we had no idea where you were.

"She then seduced one of the younger witches in some sort of ritual which enabled her to locate you, or so she claimed. According to Azurine, the young witch involved, Magdalene returned later and was in a fury. She entered Azurine's bedroom and cruelly abused her.

"We assumed her anger was fueled by her failure to find you."

Alexandra shakes her head and tells Esmeralda, "No, it wasn't because she could not locate me, it was because I eluded her grasp. The man she…the man you mentioned is a dear friend of mine. Somehow he managed to find the strength to warn me. He saved my life."

Rosslyn reaches over to take Alexandra's hand as her eyes fill with tears. Wiping them away, Alexandra says, "I will see she pays dearly for what she has done to him. He is…" unable to finish, she grips Rosslyn's hand to steady herself.

Claire says, "We all have our reasons for wanting to see Magdalene punished. She is an evil spirit with no good left in her heart."

Dawn takes the opportunity to turn the conversation back to the issue of how to proceed. "I have Simha's book. Perhaps Claire or Esmeralda can see something in it Alexandra and I have missed," she says.

Excitedly, Esmeralda asks, "Have you seen him? Is he well?"

Alexandra answers, "She did not see him. I did. He came to me on the roof of a cathedral in Cádiz. He tested me to be sure I was the one he was waiting for, then he handed me the book. I don't know if he returned to his bookstore, or if he departed for the Akashic Realm. I am sorry."

"Oh. I see," Esmeralda says. "I would have enjoyed spending time with him again. We were close once but that was many lifetimes ago. May I see the book?" she asks Dawn.

"Of course," Dawn answers placing it in her hands.

Esmeralda solemnly runs her fingers over the embossed leather cover. She smiles. "I feel him. He poured his soul into this work. A part of him will always be within it," she says.

Opening the book, she begins to read. Her eyes grow misty as she recalls her part in the events recounted.

Continuing to read, her attention is caught by the description of a creature she has never heard of.

"This passage talks about a wind daemon. Have any of you ever heard this name before?" she asks.

Alexandra excitedly replies, "No, not in those words but I know of the wind wraith. His name is Samir.

"I was told he is an ancient being, created when this planet was young. He is the only one of his kind."

Esmeralda says, "Samir? I believe I met him. He also came to our covenhome looking for you. He was traveling with two others; Jake and Aaron."

Nodding, Claire says, "Yes the three of them were together. Sadly, Magdalene murdered Aaron, but, Jake and Samir are now here together. Please read what it says."

Esmeralda reads the passage aloud.

"Today I encountered a stranger who appeared at first as a spinning column of air. He coalesced into a man-like form. His presence was announced by a sound, not unlike millions of birds singing as one. I asked his name but he refused to reveal it. 'My name is my own. I will not share it,' he said.

"I asked where he was headed. 'I am lost," he said. 'Everything that matters to me has been taken away.'

"Wanting to help, I told him he was welcome to return to my shelter and remain with me for as long as he wished. He thanked me and replied he would be grateful for the company."

Esmeralda skips ahead several pages and continues.

"The wind deamon asked that I not mention his presence to those in the convenhome. I agreed. In return he told me his story. It was a tragic tale and I felt great pity for him.

'Do not pity me, my friend. It was meant to be,' he told me, but still, I do.

Esmeralda searches for the entry which mentions Samir, if in fact, it is he, leaving Simha.

"The daemon has been sharing my shelter for many months but today he said it is time for him to travel on.

'This land has been good for me. There is great energy here. I feel it pulsing through my body as if it is

*using me as a conduit. I feel I am meant to unleash it
someday, but not for many thousands of years. For now,
I must continue my journey alone. I will never forget you
Simha.'*

"*It saddened me to see him go yet I understood.
Perhaps we will be part of one another's story again
someday.*"

Alexandra shakes her head, saying, "Why didn't I
pick up on that when I read it?"

Esmeralda tells her, "When I said a part of Simha
would always be in the book, I meant it literally. This is
a living document; one that changes depending on
circumstance and who is reading it. If Magdalene ever
gained possession of it, the letters would shrivel and die.
It would be the end of all of this precious knowledge
forever. No matter what occurs, we cannot allow her to
touch the book!"

Alexandra nods her head, saying, "I understand.
When I first opened it, I thought I would be unable to
decipher it. Then the letters moved and reshaped
themselves as I watched. When they were done, the
words were in English."

"Remarkable!" Claire says.

Alexandra says, "So, unless I am mistaken, Samir is
the lock we are searching for."

CHAPTER 63

Magdalene groans as she opens her eyes. Tom's body is unaccustomed to rapid jumps through space and time. It feels heavy and tired. Dragging the body out of bed takes all of the energy Magdalene can summon.

Showering beneath the hot pulsing water, Magdalene begins to revive. She can feel Alexandra's nearness. She senses their meeting is about to happen. Tom's body responds to Magdalene's fantasies. It longs to caress her curves; taste her flesh. His arms are reaching out but finding only empty air.

Shaking her head, she says, "Enough! It is time to rid the world of that insufferable bitch. I need to prepare myself."

Removing several vials of gem-colored liquid from her bag, she pours a few drops from each into a crystal chalice. Watching as the liquids swirl together she sees an image of Alexandra appear in the center.

"I will devour you!" she says as she gulps the sickly-sweet drink.

Tom's body reacts violently. It doubles over in pain, sweating and moaning. After a few moments, the pain subsides.

Magdalene then rubs an ointment made from Pratika blossoms over Tom's body. Watching herself in the mirror as she slowly massages the oil over his muscled chest, down his chiseled thighs, she is aroused. Wishing she could step out of his body and make love to him, she struggles to retain control.

"I can't allow myself to feel anything for you!" she shouts at the reflection. "Soon, you and your beloved Alexandra will be dead and I will, at last, be free!"

Tom struggles to break through, thinking, "You can have me. We could be together forever. You only need to find a female host. I know you have thought about it."

In a fury, Magdalene screams, "Do you think I am an imbecile? I know you are trying to trick me. I know you love Alexandra! I know your thoughts as intimately as you do!"

"Do you? Then you must know I want to make love to you. We are so close. Let me feel myself inside you. Let my arms hold you; my mouth savor you."

Grabbing her head, Magdalene tries to drown out his voice. Shouting and crying, she tells him, "Stop now!"

Focusing all her will on drowning out Tom's voice, she regains her power over him. Trembling from the exertion, she knows how close she has come to surrender.

"I will not weaken again," she screams at the face staring back at her.

CHAPTER 64

Alexandra hears a strange sound in the hall outside her room. She knows who it is.

"I think the last piece of the puzzle is in place," she announces."Claire, will you open the door for Jake and Samir?"

Claire gives her an odd look as she answers, "Of course."

Opening the door, Claire is overcome by waves of emotion hitting her from all directions. She reaches out to Jake, saying, "It is so good to see you, and you too, Samir."

Jake embraces the witch and tells her, "It's good to see you, all of you."

Gazing over Claire's shoulder he sees Alexandra but her expression is indecipherable.

The two enter the room followed by Samir. Jake is surprised to see Esmeralda. There are two unfamiliar faces as well.

Approaching one of the two, he holds out his hand. "I'm Jake."

Taking his hand Dawn smiles. "Of course you are. You are even more devilishly handsome than I anticipated. I am Dawn."

"And a glorious Dawn you are," he answers, kissing her hand.

Dawn introduces him to Oleander, who blushes as he kisses her hand as well.

Turning to Samir, he introduces the two witches.

After greeting Esmeralda, he finally approaches Alexandra.

Her heart is in her throat as she watches him coming closer. His lies hover in the air between them, but the desire to touch him, hold him again, is too powerful. He reaches out, gathers her in. She buries her face in his chest.

Stroking her hair, he chants her name. "I will never forgive myself for the pain I put you through."

Placing a hand over his mouth, she says, "It doesn't matter. None of it matters now. We are together and we have something we must do."

Pulling herself away, she turns to Samir, "I am very sorry about Gregory's death. I know he was your friend."

Samir answers, "Yes he was. Thank you."

Alexandra asks, "Do you and Jake know the part you will play today?"

Puzzled Jake says, "Part? No. What part are you talking about?"

Turning to his friend Samir answers, "I believe I am the lock to Alexandra's key. Together we will remove the curse of Eve."

"How long have you known this?" Jake asks angrily.

"Don't be angry my friend. I knew the moment I first set foot here thousands of years ago. I may not have known the exact circumstances until now, but I knew I was destined to unleash the energy held within this earth. How did you figure this out?" he asks Alexandra.

"It's in Simha's book. I didn't see it, but, Esmeralda did."

Turning to Esmeralda, Samir says, "He spoke of you often."

CHAPTER 65

Magdalene is still unable to pierce the veil hiding Alexandra's presence. Knowing she cannot return to Azurine, she contemplates finding another witch to aid her, but, senses she does not have time. Events are moving too quickly.

"Where are you and your little minions hiding?" she wonders. "And where is Lucien?"

Remembering their last conversation, she turns her energy towards France. Searching desperately, she is unable to find him. She does, however, notice a strange confluence of energy near the ruins of Savigny Abbey. Realizing any circle strong enough to hold Lucien captive would create a field like the one she is seeing, she heads for the spot outside Paris.

The ruins appear deserted at first glance but Magdalene senses this is a consequence of the veil surrounding Lucien. Conjuring his image, she feels an increasingly strong vibration. The ground begins to shake violently as if in the throes of a massive earthquake. Losing her footing, she falls to the ground. Trying to avoid the debris flying everywhere she covers her head. Then, the tremors stop.

She imagines the wind is speaking to her; calling her name. Following the sound to its source, she sees Lucien. He is in the center of a ring of stones. There are markings in the dirt surrounding the stones. Magdalene recognizes them. She knows how to break the spell and release Lucien.

Unable to see her, Lucien senses her presence. Calling out, he begs to be released from his prison.

Laughing, Magdalene asks, "And what will I get in return? I warned you not to come didn't I?"

Lucien answers, "Yes and you were right. I should have listened. Help me and I will find a willing host for you, one that would gladly accept your spirit and allow you to stay in this realm. We can be together as you have always wanted."

"Things have changed Lucien. I no longer wish to be with you. However, a willing host…young and beautiful…that would be a start. And, I want to share control of the gateway."

"So you believe the stories are true as well," Lucien says. He agrees to Magdalene's terms. Chanting the spellbreaker, she waves her arms and the circle fails. Lucien approaches Magdalene.

"Are you sure you no longer want me?" he asks, grabbing Tom's body and pulling it close.

Magdalene pushes away, saying, "I have never been more certain of anything. Once we have gained control of the passages, I want a new female body."

Lucien answers, "I will keep my word. I need your word you will not harm Alexandra."

"You have it," Magdalene replies.

"So, where is my daughter?"

Magdalene tells him, "I do not know for certain, but I believe she is in Scotland, near Rosslyn Chapel. Maybe together we can see through Lorelei's spells and find out exactly where she is."

They join hands and chant. Alexandra's image appears in the space between them.

CHAPTER 66

Asking everyone to give her a moment alone with Jake, Alexandra takes his hands in hers. Looking into black demon eyes, she says, "I love you. The trouble is I don't have a choice. Do you think that's fair?"

Jake answers, "No matter what you have been told, you have the power to break the spell if that's what you really want."

"What about you?" Alexandra asks. "Are you able to break the spell; to stop loving me?"

Shaking his head, Jake replies, "I will love you until the end of time. Even if I could break free, I wouldn't."

"Why?' Alexandra asks.

Jake doesn't get a chance to answer her. Suddenly, his hands no longer hold Alexandra's. They are grasping empty air.

Desperately, Jake cries out, "Alexandra!!"

The others come rushing in to find Jake on his knees and Alexandra no longer in the room.

"No! No, this can't be happening!" Claire screams. "Lucien, if this is your doing and you are helping Magdalene, you will pay dearly. I swear I will have your head!"

Lucien's voice fills the room. "You are in no position to threaten me," he says. "You are fortunate I have decided not to destroy you, but don't get in my way again. Alexandra is with me now and that is where she will remain!"

Rosslyn begins to weep; heartbreaking cries escape her as she realizes her friend is once again gone.

Crimson tears stream down her face, making small craters on the floor as they land. Her sorrow is hard for the others to bear.

Claire goes to her and says, "Please don't cry. We'll figure this out somehow."

Esmeralda says, "We have no time for tears. What's done cannot be undone. We need to focus all of our energy on helping Alexandra."

Samir says, "She is right. For now, we have an advantage over them. We know who the lock is, and we know where we need to go to enact the ritual of opening. They only know Alexandra is the key and Rosslyn Chapel is connected to it all somehow. We need to act quickly while we still have the upper hand."

"The upper hand? Without Alexandra we have nothing!" Jake says.

Samir turns to his friend, saying, "I will get her back. Magdalene can do little to harm me. If we all focus, maybe we can discover where Lucien and Magdalene have taken her."

They all agree it is the only option. Joining hands they concentrate on Alexandra. An image appears.

"I know this place. It is Lucien's house in New Orleans," Samir says.

"I want to go with you," Jake tells his friend.

Shaking his head, Samir tells him it is impossible.

"I can't take you. You know that."

Oleander interrupts, saying "There is nothing to argue about. While you were talking, Dawn left to fetch Alexandra."

Infuriated, Jake demands to know what gave Dawn the right to make such a decision alone.

"She loves Alexandra as much as you do; she knew there was no time for arguments. She did what had to be done to save her," she answers, angrily.

Samir tells his friend, "She's right. Now, all we can do is wait for Alexandra and Dawn to return."

"If they ever do return," Jake says. "How do we go forward if we have lost Alexandra?"

Samir tries to reassure his friend, saying, "Dawn is a powerful witch. I expect she will succeed. If she does not, we will have to carry on without them. Our focus then would have to be punishment for Lucien and Magdalene."

"We need to be sure, if Dawn fails, there is no way for Lucien and Magdalene to get to you. If they do, control of the gateways will be in their hands and it will be the end of everything we know," Jake says.

Samir solemnly agrees.

CHAPTER 67

Alexandra's vision clears and she sees her father and Tom standing together. Briefly forgetting Tom is not himself, she is overwhelmed with relief.

Falling to her knees, she says, "Tom, help me please."

Magdalene smiles, saying, "Of course I will help you Alexandra...of course."

Recognizing Magdalene at last, Alexandra looks to her father, screaming, "What are you doing with her and why have you brought me here? Do you realize she has tried to murder me several times?"

Lucien answers, "I have brought you here to protect you from those who would use your unique power with no thought for your safety. You know I won't let anyone or anything harm you. I love you."

"But you want the same thing from me as everyone else. And how can you be with that creature," Alexandra asks, pointing in Magdalene's direction, "if you really care about my well-being?"

"Magdalene rescued me from the captivity into which your friend Claire had placed me."

Concerned for Claire's safety, Alexandra asks, "Has anything happened to Claire? Did you hurt her?"

Lucien tells her, "No, she is fine. She was warned what would happen to her if she betrayed me but I could not follow through. After all, she did raise you, my daughter."

Alexandra says, "Maybe you do have feelings after all. So, what is it you want me to do? Without the lock, I can't open the passageways, and we don't know who or what the lock is."

Magdalene says, "Enough of this. I think you are lying. You need to tell us who the lock is, Alexandra!"

"I will not tell you anything," she answers.

"Then your demon will be the next to die," Magdalene says.

All emotion gone, she answers, "If that is what needs to happen to prevent the two of you from gaining control of the gateway, then, so be it."

Magdalene's features suddenly soften. Gazing at Alexandra, she reaches out and strokes her cheek.

"Alexandra, it's me, Tom. You know how much I love you. I've loved you for years. Please help your father and me. We don't want to hurt you, or anyone, we just want to open the passage. What harm is there? Isn't that what you want too?

"Forget about Jake. Magdalene will set me free and we can be together. Please," Magdalene says, taking Alexandra's hand and pulling her close. "Please help us," she begs, bending down to kiss Alexandra's waiting lips.

Feeling herself swallowed up in Tom's strong arms, Alexandra's mind is filled with images of the two of them together. Resting her head on his chest, she thinks "This feels so right. Why am I fighting? I know Tom loves me."

Jake's image slices through Magdalene's spell bringing Alexandra back to her senses. Pushing away from Tom, she reaches up and slaps him.

"You are not Tom," she spits at him. "Do what you want with me but I will never help you."

Magdalene grabs her wrist, twisting it until it comes close to snapping.

"You stupid little bitch," she says. "You and your friends are no match for me. You're coming with me and you will do what I say or watch them die one by one."

Lucien tries to intercede but Magdalene is too strong. As he reaches out to take his daughter away, she pulls out the dagger she had used on Alexandra and stabs him in the heart.

Yanking her arm out of Magdalene's grasp, Alexandra desperately searches for a weapon. She sees a sword in the corner of the room; the one Lucien had once used to stab Magdalene. Racing to pick it up, she feels Magdalene's power trying to hold her back.

Knowing she only has seconds to reach the weapon and cut off her father's head before his spirit is sent into limbo, she cries out her mother's name, begging for help.

Caught off guard, Magdalene's power eases enough for Alexandra to reach the sword. Scooping it up, she turns and decapitates her father. His spirit fills the room blinding Magdalene.

"Get out!" he tells his daughter. "Hurry!"

Weakened by the effort to save her father's spirit, Alexandra is unable to summon the strength to transport herself. Collapsing, she feels strong arms grab her before she hits the floor. She sees the eyes of Dawn.

CHAPTER 68

It is twilight when Jake, Esmeralda, Samir, Rosslyn and Claire, arrive at Rosslyn Chapel. The building is empty. The air is alive with power as if the earth is aware of what is about to happen. Esmeralda reaches out and touches the building. The stones quiver.

The wind picks up, whipping the trees into a frenzied state. Branches reach down to the ground beating out an ancient rhythm. The North Sea sings in a voice loud enough to be heard hundreds of miles away. The sky blackens then blooms with preternatural light.

Dawn and Alexandra arrive bringing with them an eerie snowfall which warms rather than chills. Jake resists the urge to rush to her side. He stands frozen while the warm flakes cover his body. Finally looking in his direction, all Alexandra sees is a spectral form, unmoving.

Walking, then running, towards him her emotions are overwhelming. Reaching out, he takes her in; holds her while she weeps for the one she has lost. Finally spent, she says, "It's time. Magdalene will be following us soon. We need to finish this."

They enter the chapel. Alexandra gasps at the astonishing sight. Carvings that have stood still for centuries are stirring; writhing and spinning as they reach for the heavens.

Samir takes her hand and they move to the center of the chapel. He begins to hum, spinning in circles around Alexandra. She feels the breath of life sucked out of her; a new force enters her. Rising up from the ground she moves in a dance as old as the universe. Her now naked body bends in ways no human body could; twisting, curling, sprouting limbs like branches from a tree.

In the midst of the maelstrom, Magdalene's arrival goes unnoticed. Silently she watches Alexandra. Tom's desire for her is so strong it appears as a flame dancing circles around her. Struggling to contain it, Magdalene cries out.

Jake rushes towards her as the ceremony reaches its conclusion. The walls of the chapel collapse. The carvings resolve into pillars framing a sea of darkness. The earth shivers as the ancient gateway opens.

Magdalene sees Jake coming and heads for the opening.

Screaming to Esmeralda to stop her, Jake makes a last desperate lunge, but he is too late. Magdalene is gone, escaping through the gateway.

Jake feels someone touching his shoulder. Turning, he sees Alexandra, but not Alexandra. She has become something more; different. In that instant, he knows he has lost her.

"Jake, I'm sorry," she says. "I love you but…"

Taking her hands in his, he says, "No need to explain my love. The world needs you. You have to help them understand what has happened. Without you, civilization could dissolve into chaos."

Tears are streaming down her face as embraces him. "Someday…"

"Please, don't say any more. I'll wait for as long as it takes."

Turning away, Alexandra calls the four witches to her side.

"We have much work to do," she tells them.

Turning to face Jake once more she reaches out and then slowly turns and walks away, surrounded by the four.

Samir holds his friend as Jake's heart-rending wail pierces the night. Finally exhausted, Jake turns to Samir.

"And so do we…" he says as they follow Magdalene into the darkness of the gateway together.